Mai
Enjoy
Eva! Stay Wilde!

WILDE FOR HER

A WILDE SECURITY NOVEL

M Burrows

TONYA
BURROWS

Previously released on Entangled's Brazen imprint —
October 2015

Entangled Publishing, LLC
2614 South Timberline Road
Suite 109
Fort Collins, CO 80525
Visit our website at www.entangledpublishing.com.

Ignite is an imprint of Entangled Publishing, LLC.

Edited by Heather Howland and Sue Winegardner
Cover design by Heather Howland
Cover art from iStock

Manufactured in the United States of America

First Edition October 2013

ignite

To my mentor, Victoria Thompson, whose advice has never steered me wrong.
And to my critique partners, Traci Douglass, Becky Watson, and Sheri Flemming. Thanks for putting up with my unpunctuality, ladies!

Chapter One

Camden Wilde felt like a suspect in a police line-up.

A suspect dressed as a Jimmy Buffet tribute band reject, but still.

Yeah, they must have been a sight, the five big, bad Wilde brothers in their Hawaiian print shirts, khaki shorts, and flip-flops, standing side-by-side under a lone palm tree on the breezy Key West beach. But, damn, did all of the wedding guests have to stare?

Jude would pay for this. Big time.

The happy groom-to-be stood beside a priest who looked like the frontman of that Jimmy Buffet tribute band. Always antsy, Jude bounced a little on his feet as a tropical version of the bridal march started, his impatience to see his bride tangible.

Who would've guessed the youngest Wilde would be the first to take the plunge? Cam certainly hadn't seen it coming, but without a doubt, it felt right. Libby was good for Jude.

Lucky bastard.

Not that Cam wanted any of this marriage shit for himself. He'd done the whole loved and lost thing once before when his parents were murdered, and he damn well wasn't gonna voluntarily sign up to put himself through that kind of pain again. He'd learned long ago he couldn't stop himself from loving, but he could protect himself by keeping his distance and keeping any relationships he had short and sweet and purely physical. Hell would be icy for ten years before he went anywhere near an altar—unless, like today, he was standing up for one of his brothers.

But him, a groom? Never happening.

Jude, on the other hand, made a damn good one, Hawaiian print shirt and all. When Libby appeared at the end of the flower-strewn wood walkway, a glowing vision in a gauzy, pale-blue dress with her arm resting in the crook of her father's, Jude went completely still and sucked in an audible breath. The look on his face could only be described as awed. He pressed his lips together, visibly fighting back emotion.

"It's official," Vaughn said under his breath. "Little brother is a complete sap."

Cam elbowed his twin in the ribs. "Don't be like that. It's good to see him happy."

"Happy's one thing," Vaughn muttered and squinted against the setting sun. "But if he starts crying, I'm gonna have to break his face on principle."

"Twins," Greer said out of the side of his mouth. "Shut up."

Cam winced. He hated when Greer called them "twins" as if they didn't each have a name. Vaughn grumbled something about "older fucking brothers" and Reece, serving as best man, sent all three of them a warning look as their conversation started drawing attention. Thankfully, not a lot. Most everyone focused on the center of the aisle, where Libby's father handed her off to a beaming Jude.

The ceremony got underway and Cam let his gaze wander over the assembled guests, searching for his "date." He found her in the last row of chairs, fidgeting in her tight-fitting sundress like she couldn't wait to get out of it.

He could help her with that.

No. He immediately shut down that line of thought. Not appropriate. Not when it came to Eva Cardoso. She'd been his partner, and even though he no longer worked on the police force, it wasn't kosher to think about her in any way but as a former co-worker and friend.

Forget that he'd been in love with her for the last five years. It still wasn't right.

She noticed him looking at her and flipped him the bird, which made him grin. That was Eva all right. All steel and fire and no social grace.

The wedding ceremony was quick and sweet. And, yeah, maybe he choked up a little bit when the priest announced the new couple. There hadn't been a Mr. and Mrs. Wilde since his parents died.

God, he wished they were here to see this. They'd both be so proud of Jude.

Cam followed his brother and new sister-in-law back down the aisle to a round of applause, his arm linked with a bridesmaid's. But when he reached the end of the runner, he broke away with a murmured apology to the woman and walked over to where Eva still sat.

"Your brother and his wife look ecstatic," she said as he approached.

"They are."

Frowning a little, she watched Jude and Libby until they disappeared into their beachside hotel, where the reception was being held. "Is it wrong to be jealous of them?"

Cam opened his mouth, but found he had no answer.

She waved a hand. "Never mind. Forget I said that."

Gladly, Cam thought and cast around for a topic that was a little less of a minefield. "I don't think I've ever seen you in a dress."

"I don't think I've ever seen you in a Hawaiian shirt," she shot back.

"That's because I don't do Hawaiian anything. It's Jude's idea of a joke."

"Well, I don't do dresses." She scowled and plucked at the skirt in disgust. "My sister bought it for me when I told her I'd be coming here for a wedding. It was either wear it or face her wrath when I get home. So just call me chicken. Bawk. Bawk."

Cam laughed but wasn't about to tell her that her sister had impeccable taste. The asymmetrical dress was just as edgy as Eva herself and the deep red color complimented the dark silk hair and bronze skin she'd inherited from her father's Brazilian roots. The fabric hugged curves she usually hid and parted to showcase a long leg when she stood.

Cam tried to keep his voice light as he reached over and flicked the end of the halter neck's tie. "Looks good."

Her dark eyes narrowed at him. "Are you trying to be funny? 'Cause I gotta warn you, I'm armed."

Armed? Where?

He looked her up and down and about swallowed his tongue at the possibilities.

Damn.

Something sparked behind her eyes. Recognition. A trace of heat. Panic. She backed away from him in a quick step, knocking into one of the folding chairs at the edge of the aisle. "Uh, we should probably go inside."

Cam shook himself and glanced around. They were the only ones left on the beach.

Inside. Where his brothers were probably waiting on him. Right.

He held out an arm. "Shall we?"

She ignored the gesture and bent over to pull off her sandals. "Will there be beer at this reception?"

He scoffed. "My brothers are here."

"Ah, good point." Her dark eyes crinkled at the corners as she grinned up at him. "Race ya in, Wilde. Winner buys first round."

She didn't give him a chance to respond, but took off like a thoroughbred, all graceful long legs with her dark hair streaming through the air.

Cam couldn't move, could only watch her, his heart pounding and his mouth as dry as the sand under his feet.

Damn.

He was so fucked.

Chapter Two

Eva weaved through the crowd gathered on the hotel's patio, her heart thundering and not from her sprint across the beach. She didn't dare look behind her to see if he was following, and that pissed her off. She needed to put on her big girl panties. Actually, at the moment, she'd be happy with *any* panties, big girl or not. The dress hadn't allowed for anything more than a thong, and she was counting down the hours until she could get out of the uncomfortable thing.

Annnd she was stalling.

Fuck it. She stole a glance over her shoulder and let out a breath of relief when all she saw was a crowd of nameless wedding guests. No Cam.

What the hell had that all been about anyway?

One moment it had been a typical conversation between her and Cam—and then it wasn't. She'd started getting weird vibes from him and had felt…hot. She'd looked at him in that ridiculous shirt with his dark hair mussed by the ocean breeze, his perpetual stubble darkened past a five o'clock shadow, that funny little quirk of a smile of his twisting his lips, and something changed. She'd had the urge to drag him up to her hotel room and put that perfectly made king-sized bed to good use. And maybe the glass enclosed shower. The sofa. The floor…

No.

What?

She brought those thoughts to a slamming halt.

She was no prude. She liked sex, and despite her recent dry spell, she liked to engage in it as often as possible. But, fuck, this was Camden Wilde she was fantasizing about. Her ex-partner. Her best friend. And she hadn't even had a drink yet!

Which was something she definitely needed to remedy. Right now.

Eva wound through the schmoozing wedding guests to the white tent set up as a reception hall. The sun had dipped below the horizon, painting the sky in bright pinks and soft purples. Huge paper globe lanterns hung from the ceiling and gave off a welcoming yellow glow. Two long tables, decorated with breezy white linen and tropical flower centerpieces set every few feet, ran side-by-side on a low wooden dais at one end of the tent with the wedding party's smaller table at the front. A few people had already taken their seats, but she didn't know anyone, so she ignored them all and continued her search for a cold alcoholic beverage. The other side of the tent was an open stretch of sand that she assumed would be the dance floor once the DJ in the corner finished setting up his equipment. Until then, a quartet played soft guitar music on another low dais. It was nice, if not a bit snooze-worthy.

But no bar.

Must be out on the patio, which explained why so many people had gathered there. Steeling herself, she turned to continue her search among the gaggle of finely dressed strangers—and nearly ran into a broad chest covered with a Hawaiian print shirt. She stumbled a little, more from dismay that Cam had found her than from surprise. His big hand caught her arm to keep her upright, and she felt none of those strange vibes from him this time. Thank God. Whatever had happened between them on the beach must have been a fluke.

"Whoa," he said. "Easy."

"Shit." She straightened and shoved his shoulder as relief and a strange sense of disappointment threaded through her. "Don't sneak up on me like that, you jerk."

"I didn't sneak. I called your name, but you didn't hear me. Cam's looking for you."

"Cam? Wait, is it refer-to-yourself-in-the-third-person-day? 'Cause Eva missed that memo." The moment the words left her mouth, she felt like a complete idiot and squeezed her eyes shut for a second. "Dammit, you're Vaughn."

He grinned, and it was eerie how close that smile resembled his twin's, except his had an edge of meanness to it that Cam's didn't. "People have been doing that all day."

She eyed him. She'd always used the twins' hair lengths to tell them apart when they were together, since Vaughn tended to let his grow long and Cam kept his shorter, but now Vaughn's was just as short and even styled the same way.

"It's because you look somewhat civilized now," she told

him.

He ran his hand through his dark hair, mussing the gelled locks on top so that they fell into his blue-gray eyes instead of continuing to lay flat. If she didn't know him any better, she'd think he was embarrassed about the haircut.

"It's just for the wedding," he said. "Libby said I looked like a thug and didn't want me scaring off her bridesmaids."

"She's a smart woman. Now, excuse me, but I need a drink." She stepped aside to go around Vaughn, but his hand still held her arm and he wasn't letting go. She looked down at his tanned fingers, then back up at him and quirked a brow.

"I kinda need my arm back."

"Yeah, in a minute."

"Got something on your mind you wanna share, big guy?"

"I don't share."

"And I'm not surprised by that. Still, I do need my arm back."

He said nothing more. She gave him her best bad cop stare and tried to wait him out, but the damn man had been a SEAL, and he had the patience to out-wait an apocalypse. There was no way she'd win this battle, so she finally gave up trying.

"All right. I'm over this pissing contest we got going on. Either let me go or you're going to be singing soprano for a while. How about that?"

He released his hold and had the grace to look a little ashamed at the red marks he'd left on her skin. "Just…be good to him or we'll have problems, got me?"

No. No, she didn't get him at all. Eva watched him stride away and shook her head, feeling as if he'd just hauled off and socked her in the jaw.

What the hell did he mean by that?

She trailed after him to the patio and watched him clap the back of a handsome dark-haired guy carrying a cane. The two bullshitted until a blond man joined them and handed the guy with the cane a bottle of beer. There was some more BS-ing, followed by another back slap for each of the two men, then Vaughn broke away from them and found his twin. Eva winced when he nodded and pointed in her direction—Cam had obviously asked if Vaughn had seen her. For all of a half second, she thought about ducking back into the crowd, but that was ridiculous. Cam was her best friend and, technically, her date for the night. She wasn't going to be able to avoid him forever.

Big girl panties, she reminded herself and plastered on a smile as Cam started toward her. He also got waylaid by the two men, but he easily excused himself from them and finally made it across the patio.

"There you are," he said and handed her one of the two bottles of beer he held. "Loser buys first round, right?"

"Right." She clinked the neck of her bottle against his. "You've gotten slow since quitting the force."

"Yeah, that's what riding a desk all day does for a guy."

And cue the awkward silence.

Minutes ticked by, and they stood side-by-side without saying a word, studying the crowd. Cam seemed to want to say something, but stopped himself and took a slug of his beer instead.

Desperate to break the silence, Eva nodded to the blond guy and the one with the cane. "Who are they? I didn't see them at the wedding."

"The one with the cane is Gabe Bristow, and the other guy's Quinn. They were in the area, so Vaughn told them to stop by the reception if they got a chance. They were on the teams with him."

That piqued her curiosity and she studied the two with renewed interest. "SEALs?"

"Used to be. Now they run a private group that specializes in hostage rescue. And the woman coming up to them?" He motioned his beer toward a woman with long, golden brown hair. Her yellow dress flowed behind her as she hurried through the crowd. "That's Gabe's wife, Audrey."

Audrey tugged on her husband's shirt and motioned for him to lower his head so she could whisper in his ear. Gabe laughed at whatever she'd said and pressed an affectionate kiss to her forehead.

Eva glanced away from the pair, only to see Jude and Libby standing hand-in-hand a short distance away, a fortified unit against the exhausting wave of well-wishers. There was so much love and trust between them, it hurt to look at.

A pang of longing struck Eva in the chest with such force it took her breath away. What was so wrong with her that she couldn't find the kind of strong, lasting relationship those two couples had?

Must be hereditary. Certain people had to be genetically predisposed to happy marriages—the kinds of people raised in normal households, who had soccer moms and doting fathers. Not people like Eva, raised by an irresponsible mother who fell for whatever loser showed her the least bit of attention. Then one day the loser would leave and Katrina Bremer would fall further into depression and drugs until the next one came along. After witnessing what each new heartbreak did to her mother year after year, Eva supposed she'd never be able to give up enough control to put her own heart in a man's hands.

Cam's hand landed on her shoulder, startling her back to the present, and awareness seeped from the skin under his palm into her chest and belly, warming her from the inside out.

Oh, shit. Not this again.

He was her best friend. Best. Friend. She wasn't supposed to light up like a firework every time he touched her. What the fuck was wrong with her?

She sidled a casual step away from him and took a long drink of her beer. Cam started to say something, but Jude and Libby had finally made it over to them. With an easy smile, he turned and embraced his new sister-in-law, then gave his brother a few solid thumps on the back. Niceties out of the way, Jude's smile slipped a little, and he motioned to his brother to lean in as if he was about to tell a secret.

Uh-oh. Something was up.

"What's wrong?" Cam asked.

And he was ready to jump into the situation with both feet. It was such a Cam thing to do that Eva had to bite back her smile.

Jude hesitated and exchanged glances with his wife, who nodded encouragement. He tilted his head, indicating the beach. "Seth's here," he said as if that explained everything. But judging by Cam's wince, it was enough information for him.

Eva scanned the water's edge and spotted the lone figure standing on the beach, staring out over the ocean.

"I'm worried," Jude admitted. "He won't say it, but he's having trouble with all the noise and people. He's determined to stay and torture himself even though I told him he's not going to offend us if he ducks out early. He was here for the ceremony, which was more than enough. Can you go talk to him? Convince him to go home and take it easy? I tried, Gabe and Quinn both tried. Even Audrey tried, but the stubborn jackass won't listen to any of us."

"What makes you think I'll be able to change his mind?" Cam said.

"If he'll talk to anyone, it will be you. Everyone talks to you."

That was true. Although Eva had no idea what was going on, if anyone could fix the problem this Seth guy was having, it would be Cam.

"All right," Cam said, handing his empty to Jude. "I'll give it a shot."

Eva followed him to the end of the boardwalk, where he kicked off his flip flops, then peeled out of the gaudy Hawaiian print shirt, revealing the white tank top he wore underneath and the elaborate tribal tattoo that covered most of his right shoulder. He pulled out the linings of his shorts pockets as visual proof he had nothing on him. She'd seen him do this many times before and, like all of the other times, adrenaline spilled into her blood, kicking up her heartbeat.

"Is this guy dangerous?" she asked.

"Only to himself." He handed her his shirt. "He has PTSD. He's working hard at overcoming it, but he still has rough days."

"So what are you going to do?"

"Just talk to him." He turned toward the beach, but Eva

caught his hand and gave it a quick squeeze.

"Be careful."

His lips quirked in his funny little smile and he squeezed her hand back before releasing her. "Hang back, okay? I don't want to spook him."

• • •

Cam snagged a bottle of beer from a passing waiter, then walked down to the beach and settled against a palm tree several feet away from Seth. He popped the cap off his bottle and took a long drink. It wasn't his favorite kind—too light for a guy who preferred stouts thick enough to chew—but that didn't matter. The whole point of drinking it was to put Seth at ease. No big deal. Just someone out on the beach to watch the sunset with a beer. It also gave Seth the op- portunity to start the dialogue. People abhor silence. It was human nature to seek to fill it, and it always worked like a charm when you wanted someone to talk.

Seth was no exception.

"So they're sending the hostage negotiator now?" Seth's voice was low and rusty, as if his vocal chords didn't get a daily workout. He wore the hood of his sweatshirt up despite the humid night and wouldn't look in Cam's direction, kept his gaze focused on the ocean.

Cam shrugged. "They're all worried about you."

"I'm not going to hurt myself," he said after several beats. "I didn't live through hell to kill myself now. And I'm not going to go all ape-shit and start picking people off with my rifle from the lighthouse or something."

"That's good to know."

"I'm not crazy."

Cam laughed. "C'mon, Jude's your best friend. You expect me to believe that line of bullshit? You have to be a little crazy to hang out with him."

The corner of Seth's mouth twitched upward. "He used to tell me stories about you and Vaughn when we were deployed."

"He used to tell us stories about *you* when he was home."

"He blames himself for what happened to me."

A vice of guilt clamped briefly around Cam's heart and he took a deep breath to loosen it. "Jude blames himself for a lot of things that aren't his fault. It's just the kind of guy he is. He takes everything to heart."

"I know. It's…nice to see him happy."

"It is."

The tension seeped out of Seth's shoulders. "I just wanted to come here and wish Jude and Libby well. Say congrats, maybe toast the newlyweds like a normal best man. He asked me to stand up for him, you know?"

"Yeah, he mentioned that."

"I wanted to, but…I couldn't." His fists balled inside the front pocket of his hoodie. "I'm so fucking sick of being afraid. I'm tired of worrying I won't be able to keep the people I care about safe."

Oh damn. Didn't that hit a little too close to home for comfort? "Yeah," Cam said softly. "I get that."

Seth glanced over and lowered the hood of his sweatshirt. Stubble covered his head, so short his hair color was hard to judge. A thin white scar started at the edge of his hairline, cut across his forehead and the bridge of his nose, and ended at the corner of his eye, but that one was nothing compare to

the ragged ridges of scar tissue on his neck peeking out from
under the collar of his sweatshirt.

"You know, people always say they get it. Usually, it's
just words. Hollow. How come I feel like you mean it?"

Cam tore his gaze away from the scars and stared out
over the water, his mind kicking up all kinds of gut-wrenching
images of Seth with his neck slashed open. Beaten. Tortured.
Brutalized.

And then, in a sickening twist of his imagination, Seth's
face morphed into Jude's.

It could have been Jude in that prison camp. Hell, if he
hadn't gotten dangerously ill right before the mission that
landed Seth in that horrible place, it *would have* been Jude.

And Cam would have been stuck stateside, unable to
do a damn thing to protect his baby brother. Helpless, just
like when he'd been eleven and his entire world crumbled
out from under his feet after a senseless act of violence left
the five young Wilde boys orphaned. They had lost so much
more than their parents that day. They'd lost their home,
their sense of security. And Cam had lived every second
since then terrified it would all happen again.

Seth was still staring at him, and he had the strangest
sense those blue eyes could see through him. The silence
started to get too thick. Yeah, he wasn't any more immune
to the silent treatment than the next Joe Schmo.

"So," he said after another long drink of the too-light
beer. "Jude's glad you came, but he doesn't want you staying
if it makes you uncomfortable."

"I know."

"Do you need a ride home?"

Seth heaved out a breath. "Yeah. I guess I'm not ready

for this yet."

"All right. You wanna stay here until I get my keys?"

He nodded and up came the hood again.

Cam pushed away from the tree and emptied the rest of his beer out in the sand. "I'll be back in a few." He didn't wait for a reply and walked toward Eva on the boardwalk, depositing the empty in a bin on his way.

"What happened down there?" she asked and handed back his Hawaiian shirt. "You look a little rattled."

Only she would see the slight tremor in his hands that gave away how much that encounter had upset him.

Cam slid into the shirt and buttoned it. "He has a house not too far from here. I'm going to take him home so he can regain his bearings without all this noise and confusion around him. Cover for me, will ya?"

She rubbed a hand down his bicep in a friendly caress that wasn't the least bit sexual, and yet his balls tightened at the skin-to-skin contact. She looked too good in that damn dress, with her hair loose and wavy with wilted curls…

"I'll have a Guinness waiting for you when you get back," she said.

Cam gave himself a mental slap. This was Eva. *Eva.* In other words, off limits for naked fantasies. Fuck, how many more times would he have to remind himself of that tonight? Usually, when it came to her, he had better control over his urges. He'd spent the last five years reigning them in, after all. "Uh, yeah. Thanks. I just drank half a Corona, so I'm going to need it."

She made a face. "You actually drank half a bottle of that cat piss?"

"It was for a good cause."

"Aw, my hero. I'll have two glasses of Guinness waiting then."

"Have I told you lately that I love you?" he crooned in his best Rod Stewart impression.

She rolled her eyes. "Christ. I'm never singing karaoke with you again."

Cam laughed, and it felt good, releasing some of the tension from seeing Seth's scars. He'd talked her into karaoke a few weekends ago when some of his Air Force buddies were in town, and he'd made a complete ass out of himself, much to her horror. Her refusal to sing that night after she'd accepted his dare had resulted in her coming to Key West as his plus one for the wedding. Now he was getting a kick out of breaking into random song just to needle her.

"Hey, at least I never back down from a bet."

She flipped him off, and Cam found himself smiling as he ducked into the hotel's lobby.

Chapter Three

Most of the guests had taken their dinner seats by the time Eva made it back to the reception. Laughter and the faint clink of silverware mingled with the guitar music from under the tent. She watched the happy, glittering crowd for a moment, marveled at how they all appeared at ease as they chatted over drinks and appetizers. She should join them and play her part as one of the groomsman's "dates" but…

Yeah, no.

Still barefoot, she about faced and strode into the hotel lobby, intent on finally finding the bar. She had no idea where her sandals had gone, only vaguely remembered setting them down somewhere. Didn't matter. It wasn't as if she planned on wearing those toe-crushing torture contraptions ever again.

Signs pointed the way across the lobby to a dimly lit lounge packed with other hotel patrons. She imagined there was a bar set up specifically for the wedding guests, but this was more her speed anyway: Dark and a little cramped with TVs lining the oak bar tuned to the latest football highlights. It reminded her of Maguire's, the Irish pub several blocks over from the police station, where a lot of cops hung out after their shifts. It was her and Cam's favorite hangout, and this place gave her a comforting sense of familiarity as she parked it on a padded stool and flagged the bartender, who wore the brightest neon orange shirt she'd ever seen. He practically looked radioactive and his smile was just as bright. He chatted her up as he pulled two pints of Guinness with perfect white foamy heads. After the first sip had her wiping foam from her upper lip, she supposed she could forgive him for searing her eyeballs with his choice of clothing.

Still, homesickness tugged at her.

Key West was like a carnival: wild and unpredictable, full of bright colors and strange people and fun house mirrors reflecting a distorted, margarita-soaked version of reality. It was fun to get caught up in the whirlwind of it—until you started to get nauseous from all the spinning.

Man, she missed D.C. and grumpy old Rick Maguire, who never wore neon and only "chatted" when he wanted to complain about the president's newest transgressions. At the moment, she wasn't even sure why she'd agreed to come here. Well, except for the fact that she lost a bet. And she had a really hard time saying no to Camden Wilde.

Thank God she was leaving tomorrow.

Eva set the second pint of Guinness in front of the empty stool beside her. Cam wouldn't have any trouble finding her when he got back, and she was a woman of her word. Besides, he deserved it. There was something about the man that people instinctively trusted. Even she had trusted him from the get go, and she wasn't one to trust blindly. She'd been new to homicide, fresh out of a two-year stint with narcotics, and nervous that she wouldn't be taken seriously as a woman in the all-male squad. But the moment she set her bag down on her new desk, Cam had slid his chair across the aisle between their desks and offered her a carrot stick.

"Carrot stick?" she'd echoed like a dunce, unsure that she'd heard him right and leery that he might be playing a prank on the noob.

He shrugged and took a bite of one. "Better than a cancer stick. I'm trying to quit."

They caught their first new case together that afternoon. A man had shot and killed his girlfriend and barricaded himself inside an apartment with the couple's newborn daughter. Eva soon learned Cam was the only certified negotiator in their squad, a former member of the Emergency Response Team. That was the first time she'd ever seen him turn his pockets inside out and walk into the lion's den with his hands held up.

How could you not trust the guy?

"Eva?"

Yanked out of her reminiscence, she half-turned in her seat, expecting to see Cam and ready to congratulate him on a job well done. But then the voice registered like a sucker punch, and she whipped around. Not Cam. Definitely not Cam.

Oh, God, that voice. Like a sensual rasp of velvet over her nerve endings.

Please, no. It can't be him. She was hundreds of miles from D.C. It just couldn't be—

The familiar scent of Preston Linz surrounded her. His cologne hinted at coffee, wood, and citrus fruits, and she used to love the smell. Now it made her slightly nauseous. Was he still using the same bottle she'd bought him last year for Christmas?

"Holy cow," he said, ever the politician, always so careful about not swearing in public. "It is you. I almost didn't recognize you in that dress. Wow. You look gorgeous."

She didn't bother with a smile. "What the hell are you doing here?"

His eyebrows climbed toward his hairline. He used to have a slightly unruly mop of sandy blond hair, but now he wore it cut and styled in a gelled sweep away from his handsome, narrow face.

"C'mon, Eva. Is that any way to greet an old friend?"

"We're not friends," she said unequivocally. "We're exes. Big difference."

His polished smile dropped into a scowl. "I thought we agreed to be civil about everything."

"Yeah, in D.C. We crossed state lines, so that verbal agreement is now void." With that, she chose a TV at random and pretended to be interested in the scrolling football highlights as she sipped her beer. Hmm. The Patriots tromped the Bills. No surprise there. The Steelers won against the Titans in overtime. And, dammit, the Redskins got their asses handed to them by the Packers. Fucking Redskins.

"Eva…" Preston caught her wrist as she reached for her glass. He tugged until she faced him, and hurt shown in his dark eyes.

Okay, so she was being childish. They'd been splitsville for six months now. Time to move on, right? Besides, deep in her heart, she knew he'd made the right call by ending their two-year relationship. They'd met at the YMCA five years ago, where they both swam laps in the morning, and she'd originally spurned his advances. She hadn't been looking for a relationship, didn't want to tie her happiness and self-worth to a man like her mother had, but that didn't deter him. He'd worked at her for years, winning her over little by little until a tiny, forbidden hope flared that maybe—just maybe—he'd be the one to give her the one thing she'd never had: a steady, stable family.

Things had started off great between them. They had a lot of the same interests. They both enjoyed the Nationals and had gone to as many ballgames as they were able to fit into their busy schedules. Which, unfortunately, wasn't many. They enjoyed the same kinds of movies and music— blow 'em up action flicks and country. They both loved to camp and hike—and, boy, had they gone on some crazy trips together to the backwoods of West Virginia, the memories of which still made her smile. She had liked spending time with Preston. He was good in bed and also easy to get along with outside the bedroom. He was a comfortable fit. Maybe too comfortable and too easy, because they had hardly ever fought. He never got angry and retreated from her when she did. Even their break-up had been half-hearted.

But despite how seemingly well-suited they were for each other, there were two big obstacles to them ever having a happily ever after. One: Preston was politically ambitious. The harder he worked to climb the unstable ladder of D.C. politics, the less she felt like she knew him. He stopped suggesting camping trips and started asking her to black tie social events. He started griping about her job, which had never bothered him before. As time went on, they'd spent less and less of it together.

And two: He'd recently confessed to her that he didn't want to get married. Ever. And she'd promised herself a long time ago that if she was going to do the whole relationship thing—which she wasn't anymore; she'd sworn off men six months ago—but *if* she wanted a relationship, she would do it all in the right order. Dating, engagement, wedding, honeymoon, then maybe a kid or two a few years down the road, once they were settled. Exactly the opposite of what every woman in her family had done. She'd seen her mother and sister both go through enough men to start their own football teams, and she wanted no part in that. It was either the whole shebang or nothing at all.

So, yeah, Preston had been right to end things. It still stung, but he'd been right.

She sighed and shook off his grasp. "Okay, Preston. I'm sorry for being bitchy. You know how I get when I'm forced to wear a dress and be social."

He gave a slight wince at the swear word and glanced around. Hah. Some things never change. She rolled her eyes, pretending that his distaste for cursing wasn't somewhat adorable. She always used to tease him about it.

"It's a nice dress," he offered. "Let me guess, Shelby bought it?"

She nodded and picked up her beer. "When I told her I'd been invited to a wedding here, she went all fashionista on me. Even forced me to go shopping and try shit on. I barely managed to talk her out of buying me a sequined prom-bomb in feisty fuchsia."

This time he did a better job at hiding his wince with a

smile. "Wedding? Me, too. Well, in a way. I'm vacationing with a friend who's in wedding a party. Popular destination isn't it? I've seen several brides since I got here. Anyone I know?"

"Cam's brother got hitched."

His smile didn't slip, but his face tightened the way it always had whenever Cam came up in conversation. "And how is Camden? I heard through the grapevine that he left MPD to become a private investigator."

The way he said "private investigator" suggested he thought about as highly of the profession as he did a wad of chewed gum on the bottom of his loafer. Not that she could really blame him for his disdain. She'd had a similar reaction when Cam first told her his plans to leave their tight-knit homicide squad. Still, she felt the need to defend Cam and his brothers.

"Wilde Security is actually doing quite well."

"So I've heard," Preston said. "The Pruitts are old money. I'm sure they paid the Wilde brothers handsomely for clearing up that whole stalker incident earlier this year."

"And they ended up with a son-in-law in Jude Wilde," she pointed out.

"Which I'm sure Colonel Pruitt was absolutely thrilled about." The sarcasm in his statement was thick enough to cut with a chainsaw, suggesting Colonel Elliot Pruitt was not a-okay with the marriage, although he seemed happy enough when he walked his daughter down the aisle. But even if he'd been putting on a front for the benefit of the wedding guests, what did it matter? Eva liked Libby well enough and Jude was like a little brother to her, but their family drama was none of her—or anyone else's—business.

Between her mother and Shelby, she had enough of her own drama, thanks.

Time for a subject change. "So where's your friend?"

"Doing the wedding thing. I flew down on a whim yesterday without RSVPing, so I'm left to entertain myself for the evening. Shouldn't you be at your wedding?"

"Cam had to leave for a few minutes. I'll go back when he returns. Until then..." She lifted her drink in a silent toast. "Bottoms up."

"You always could put away alcohol like no woman I've ever met."

Part of her wished that had been a dig at her lack of femininity so she'd have an excuse to be snotty and dismiss him, but his tone of voice painted it as a compliment.

"Thanks." She scanned the bar, mentally urging Cam to hurry up. She was over making polite conversation. Of course, once he got back, she'd have to go make polite conversation with the wedding guests, so it was really a lose-lose kind of night.

She knocked back the rest of her Guinness and caught the bartender's attention for another. She slid Cam's drink in front of her and decided to put the fresh one in its place.

Christ, where was Cam?

As if her thoughts conjured him, he appeared in the doorway, holding the door open for one of Libby's bridesmaids—the one he'd escorted down the aisle after the ceremony. With streaky brown hair and big blue eyes, she was the kind of gorgeous woman who made beauty look effortless. Her blue wrap dress accentuated a body that probably made men drop to their knees in front of her and pledge their undying devotion. Cam was certainly falling all over himself to help her through the door. Because, God forbid, she might break a nail if she had to open the damn thing herself.

Whoa.

Eva shifted her gaze away from them and stared into her pint, watching the foam slide down the side of the glass. Where had those bitter thoughts come from? So what if Cam wanted to hold the door for the woman. So what if he flirted a bit. So what if he wanted to fuck her. As a matter of fact, good for him if he did. Eva couldn't recall the last time he'd been on a date and the hand and lotion routine was probably getting as old for him as her vibrator was for her.

Heat flushed under her skin at a vivid mental image of Cam naked, splayed out on a bed with his head thrown back against a pillow, his chest heaving with each breath, his skin sweat-slicked, his hand closed around his cock, sliding up and down…

Double whoa.

Did the bartender turn off the A/C? Must have because it was getting really freakin' hot in here, and it absolutely had nothing to do with the completely verboten thought of her best friend naked, giving himself a hand job. She snatched up her beer and gulped it, trying to cool her parched throat.

The scent of Cam's favorite cinnamon gum surrounded her as he touched her shoulder, and she gazed down at his hand in a daze. She never noticed the size of it before—wide with a dusting of dark hair over the back. His long, tanned fingers engulfed her whole shoulder and she was in no way considered a petite woman. If anything, her shoulders were too wide from years of religious lap swimming. But as his fingers tightened in concern and she felt his leashed strength, she realized just how small she was compared to him. Despite all of the hours she spent in the gym, he could still hurt her without breaking a sweat if he wanted to. She suddenly hated him for that fact of biology almost as much as she was fascinated by it.

"You okay?" he asked.

She opened her mouth to answer, but no sound emerged. Oh. Yeah. Breathing was a good thing. She exhaled softly so as not to draw attention to the fact she'd been holding her breath, but his eyes narrowed and zeroed in on Preston over the top of her head.

"Linz," he said with a distinct chill in the curt greeting.

Shit. He thought Preston had upset her. If he only knew where her thoughts had truly been...

"Wilde," Preston said in the exact same cold tone, and then silence descended. The two men locked stares in their own private game of chicken. They'd never liked each other, and the end of her and Preston's relationship had meant the end of any semblance of civility between them.

Eva returned her attention to her beer and the TVs, fully intending to ignore them both and leave them to do their macho thing, but a flash of blue fabric out of the corner of her eye caught her attention. She turned on her stool to see the bridesmaid standing beside Preston, her blue eyes tracking from Preston to Cam and back. The woman's beauty was even more stunning up close than it had been from across the room. Next to her, Eva felt like a kid playing make believe with her mother's clothes and make-up.

"Oh, for godssakes." The bridesmaid finally leaned between the men and held out a manicured hand in greeting. "If I wait for one of these He-men to introduce me, we'll be standing here all day. I'm Lark Warren, Preston's fiancée."

The seat dropped out from under Eva's ass and the room started a sickening whirl. Her stomach clenched as pain cleaved open the wound in her heart that had just barely healed.

"Fiancée?" she heard herself ask, but her voice sounded muffled like she was whispering through the roar of a waterfall.

"It's all very recent." Lark looped her arm through Preston's and gave a dazzling smile. The ring on her finger caught and reflected the dim light from over the bar. "We've only been together about eight months, but when it's right, it's right."

Eight months? Eva shut her eyes at the wash of fresh new pain, bitter and ice cold. Their relationship had ended only six months ago.

He'd cheated.

No wonder he'd wanted out. It had never been a case of him not wanting to marry—he just hadn't wanted to marry *her*.

Cam's hand left her shoulder, slid around her waist to keep her upright, and somehow, that gave her the fortification she needed to open her eyes and face Lark again.

The woman who was everything she wasn't.

Chapter Four

Goddammit.

Cam tried to catch Lark's gaze and motioned for her to ix-nay the marriage talk, but she continued to blithely crush Eva's heart into dust with each innocent word out of her mouth. He didn't think she was intentionally being cruel. She just had no fucking idea that the woman sitting across from her in stone-faced silence was once hoping for that ring, that wedding, and a ridiculous fairy tale happily ever after.

Goddamn Preston Linz.

Eva's chest started heaving. He had no doubt she was on the verge of either punching something or breaking down and, shit, she wouldn't forgive herself if she did either in front of her asshole ex. Cam wrapped his arm tighter around her and tucked her against his side, offering what little comfort he could. She was like an icicle beside him, cold and so very fragile.

She stared at her ex, but the hurt and betrayal Cam knew she was feeling was buried so far under the ice that nobody else saw it.

At least Preston the Bastard had the grace to look ashamed. He stood up so fast, his stool scraped across the floor. "You should get back to the reception, honey." He tugged on Lark's hand. "I'll be upstairs when you're done."

Coward. Cam's fingers curled into a fist and he worked to loosen them, although the ball-less, lying, cheating jackass deserved nothing more than to lose a few teeth—especially since he was now scowling at the way Cam's arm wrapped protectively around Eva. Like he still had any right to her at all. Hah.

But that flash of jealousy gave Cam an excellent idea. He shifted behind Eva and wrapped his other arm around her, pulling her back against him and nuzzling her hair before breathing in her ear, "Play along."

Her spine stiffened, but only for a split second before she caught on to his game. She relaxed against him and reached back to tangle her fingers in his hair in a possessive way that all but screamed, "*Mine!*" The gentle tug at his scalp sent blood rushing southward.

Damn. Maybe this wasn't such a great idea after all.

"Congratulations," she said to Lark, and give the lady an Oscar because she sounded genuinely happy for the couple. "Do you have a date set? I've always wanted a spring wedding myself, but if *someone* doesn't ask me soon, we're not going to have time to plan."

Cam summoned up his most indulgent smile. "I'm working up to it."

"Oh my God," Lark said. "I had no idea you two were

a couple."

"We've kept it quiet." Eva dropped her hand from his hair to stroke her fingers affectionately back and forth over his forearm. "We used to work together and our relationship wasn't exactly condoned."

"But now that I'm no longer with MPD, there's no need for secrecy anymore," Cam added and watched Preston do the mental calculations. The guy's eyes bugged as he realized that, according to their fictional timeline, Eva had been "cheating" on him at the same time he had been seeing Lark behind her back.

Yeah, pal, how do you like that little taste of your own medicine? Going down hard, isn't it?

"I need to go," Preston said. "I have a bit of work to do and Lark, shouldn't you be getting back to the wedding?"

"You're right, I should." She smiled and lifted her face for a goodbye kiss.

Cam sure as hell didn't want Eva seeing that, so he spun her seat around to face him and did the first thing that came to mind—he dropped his mouth to hers.

He almost thought she'd shove him away. Maybe punch him for good measure. But she didn't. In fact, she didn't offer any resistance at all. She looped her arms around his neck and threw herself into the kiss with the same ferocity that she did everything else. It was the kind of kiss that promised x-rated fun in his future, and the semi-erection he'd been fighting all day demanded instant attention. A distant part of his consciousness noticed Lark dragging away her very dismayed fiancé—but then he didn't give a damn anymore and shut his eyes, melting into the kiss and giving as good as he got. Eva's tongue met and parried with his, fighting for dominance, and a thrill rippled through him. Going to bed with her wouldn't be sweet or gentle. It would be more like hand to hand combat, with each of them fighting to come out on top.

It was exactly what he'd always wanted from her.

Wait. What was he thinking? This kiss was a ruse. It wasn't real. He was simply doing her a favor, being a good friend by helping her make her ex jealous to soothe her wounded pride.

Fuck, he really hated being stuck in the *friend* category.

Cam opened his eyes to stare down at her. It took another moment before Eva realized he'd stopped participating in the fake kiss and she pulled away, a question in her caramel colored eyes.

"They're gone now," he said by way of explanation, his voice far rougher than it should have been for a *friend*.

"Oh." Her lips, wet from the kiss, parted on a soft exhale and his cock jumped, pressing painfully against the fly of his shorts. He needed to reach down and adjust things to make it more comfortable, but—well, this was Eva. He'd spent the last five years hiding this kind of reaction from her, and the last thing he wanted was to draw attention to it.

She dropped her hands from his shoulders and spun toward the bar. "Okay, that was weird."

Cam winced. Kissing her had been a lot of things, but for him, weird was nowhere on that list. "Yeah. Weird. Right." He sat down on the stool beside her and took the opportunity to do some below-the-belt adjusting. "I need a shot of something strong. Want a shot?"

She nodded, but wouldn't look at him. Goddammit.

Cam told the bartender to surprise them. Neither he nor

Eva said anything more until two blood-red shots landed in front of them a few minutes later. In unison, they picked up the glasses, clinked the rims, tapped the bottoms on the bar, and downed the contents in their usual ritual. Cam caught a nasty whiff of the concoction as he raised it to his mouth, but by the time he realized it was essentially alcoholic hot sauce, it was already down his throat. It scorched his esophagus like liquid fire laced with chili peppers and he gagged.

"Oh, what the fuck was that?" Eva gasped, sticking out her tongue and breathing like a Lamaze student.

Tears leaked out of Cam's eyes and he made a grab for one of the glasses of water the laughing bartender set down in front of them. The water did little to cool the nuclear explosion in his mouth, and he couldn't form a reply.

"It's called a Prairie Fire," the bartender said.

"Shit," Cam managed after gulping down most of the water on one breath. "Why didn't you warn us, man?"

The bartender shrugged. "Entertainment. You wanted a surprise." He hooked a thumb over his shoulder at a list of twelve shots scrawled on a chalkboard. "And not many people order off the specials list."

"They don't, huh?" Eva fished an ice cube out of her glass and slid Cam a challenging sideways glance as she crunched it. Like that, the weirdness of the last few minutes evaporated and she was Eva, his former partner and best friend, again.

And he knew that look.

"No." He held up his hands. "We're not going there."

"Oh, I'm so going there. Betcha won't try another *special*."

Cam grumbled. Growing up with a twin, two older

brothers, and one younger, dares had been a way of life. He'd lose his man card if he ever backed down from a bet, not to mention get razzed from within an inch of his life—and Eva knew this, too. Damn woman.

But…she was laughing now, which meant she wasn't thinking about Preston Linz. She was angling for a distraction, and if he had to kill his liver to keep her from beating herself up over that guy, then so be it. "What kind of bet are we talking?"

"Fifty bucks. We each pick three shots for the other and the first to refuse one loses."

"Fine. Do your worst."

"I plan on it." Eva studied the list, then ordered a Four Horsemen at the bartender's recommendation. The shot look innocuous enough when it arrived. Just a squat glass with dark, goldish-brown liquor in it.

Eva frowned at it, apparently disappointed that it wasn't flame red and reeking of hot sauce. "That doesn't look so bad."

Yeah, easy for her to say. She wasn't the one drinking it. Any shot called the Four Horsemen had to be damn near apocalyptic.

Cam fortified himself before picking up the glass. He raised it in a toast to her, tapped the bottom on the bar, and with a shake of his head at his stupidity, he knocked it back. And shuddered.

"Oh. Oh, fuck. It's like lighter fluid."

Eva grinned. "Your eyes are tearing up again."

He narrowed his eyes at her, but the glare lost some of its effect since it squeezed a few tears out to roll down his cheeks. He wiped them away with the back of his hand and banged the glass down with a triumphant *thunk*. "Go ahead and yuck it up now. You just wait."

Eva held her hand up, palm out, and curled her fingers twice in a Matrix-style *bring it* gesture.

Yeah, it was on. He took his time to study every alcoholic horror the chalkboard had to offer, then finally decided on something called a Cement Mixer.

Eva's smile widened when the bartender cheerily poured a shot of Bailey's. "Hah. I love Bailey's."

Cam said nothing, just tilted his head to draw her attention back to what the bartender was doing. The man poured lime juice into the Bailey's and the liqueur immediately started to curdle. Eva winced and reached for the shot like someone would reach into a snake pit. She gave him a pleading look, but he wasn't about to take pity now. Not when the apocalyptic lighter fluid shot was still burning a hole in the lining of his stomach.

He mimed taking the shot. "Bottoms up or pay up."

"Oh, I hate you," she said, then downed it. Or at least tried to, but its consistency was indeed like cement and she ended up chewing it, making faces the whole time.

Cam laughed. "Hey, this was your idea."

"I'm gonna get you for this one," she mumbled and finally managed to force the Cement Mixer down her throat.

The game quickly devolved from there, ending with Eva choking down a shot called Motor Oil, which she declared aptly named because it did taste like the black gunk that came out of a car long overdue for an oil change. Cam finished on some nasty concoction of Jägermeister and a dollop of warm mayonnaise and the slimy consistency had him coughing the moment it hit the back of his throat.

Eva laughed so hard she snorted and covered her mouth with her hand. "The look on your face… Oh, wait, where's your phone? I need a record of this."

She reached across the space between them and stuck her hand in his right front pocket, where he always kept his phone. With the alcohol in his system already warming him from the inside out, he thought he might burst into flames at the feel of her hand brushing against his thigh—and other, *harder* things. He started fantasizing about her closing her hand around his cock and giving it a hard stroke right there under the overhang of the bar—and that didn't help his situation any. He really should be thinking about baseball. Or golf. That was a perfectly unexciting sport. Except her fingers were right there, and he found himself unable to focus on anything but the sensation of her lingering touch. He tried to suppress the groan gathering in his chest, but didn't quite manage it.

Eva stared up at him, her eyes glazed and lids heavy. Her lips parted on a soft, shaky exhale, her fingers flexed, and anticipation rocketed up his shaft. Just a few more centimeters over…

After a long, uncertain moment, she withdrew her hand. He missed the contact instantly.

Hello, awkward silence. And they had been doing so well, too.

"We should get back to the wedding," she said a bit breathlessly and wobbled to her feet.

The wedding. Right. But, damn, with the way she was looking at him, all but stripping him with her eyes…

He stood, but didn't make any move to leave. Instead, he stepped into her personal space, his heart pounding so hard he wouldn't have been surprised if everyone in the bar could hear it. His fingers trembled a little as he flicked the tie of her halter top off her shoulder. "Are you sure?"

She glanced toward the door and winced. "No. I really don't want to go back there."

"Me, either," he admitted and leaned closer.

Eva titled her head back, her lips half parted. Maybe this was it. Maybe she'd finally give in to the sexual tension that had always been on a low simmer between them. Maybe—

She backed up a step. "I'm going to call it a night, but you should probably go back to the reception. It is your brother's wedding, after all."

Damn. Damn. Damn.

Nodding, Cam ruthlessly squashed the surge of disappointment and stepped back. "Let me pay our tab, then I'll walk you up."

"I'm a big girl, Wilde. Can take care of myself." She rubbed her thumb across his jaw, then patted his cheek. "They even let me carry a gun and everything."

Which reminded him that she was supposedly carrying a firearm somewhere under her dress, and his gaze dropped down her body. A surge of giddy lightheadedness combined with the muffled buzz of alcohol had him grabbing the bar to steady himself.

Eva turned to stroll away, but ruined her exit by wobbling dangerously after a few steps. He launched forward and caught her around the waist before she toppled, but his sense of balance was just as wonky, and they both nearly tumbled into a laughing heap on the floor.

"I'm good. I'm good," she gasped once they righted themselves. She pushed him away but didn't brace herself for when he let go and ended up flailing around like Kermit the Frog before he caught her again.

He stifled a laugh. "No, you're not. You can't possibly be because I'm buzzing pretty good, and I have at least seventy pounds on you."

"Psh. Seventy pounds or not, I can drink you under the table any day and we both know it."

Not this time. One of those shots had hit her really fucking hard. "Just let me be the gentleman my mom raised me to be, okay? She would roll over in her grave if I didn't make sure you got back to your room after letting you get this drunk."

"You didn't let me…drunk. No, wait." Realizing she'd totally slurred that sentence, she shook her head and straightened her shoulders with as much dignity as she could muster. She chose her next words more carefully. "I have a little buzz, that's all." Then she giggled, which told him everything he needed to know about how drunk she really was. Eva never giggled. "Those shots were horrible, weren't they?"

"The Jäger and mayonnaise was a particularly revolting choice," he said and gave the bartender his room number to have the tab added to his bill. He stuffed a twenty in the tip jar as he half-wobbled, half-carried Eva out the door to the elevators in the lobby.

Yeah, pretty sure the floor wasn't supposed to ebb and flow like the ocean tide. He was really going to hate himself come morning.

"Couldn't have been any worse than the Bailey's and lime juice," Eva said and jabbed the elevator's up button. "I gotta give you kudos for that one. I've never had to chew a shot anymore. No, before. I meant before."

"Yeah, I knew what you meant."

She smiled up at him. "That's 'cause you're fluent in Eva Speak."

Damn, he wanted to kiss her. It wouldn't take much with her upturned face right there, her mouth mere inches away. All he had to do was drop his head and—

The elevator doors opened and someone cleared his throat. Cam's head whipped up, which made the room spin around him, and it took a long moment to focus on his twin standing in the elevator.

Vaughn scowled at the two of them and stepped out of the car. "Where the hell have you been all night? When you didn't return, Reece started panicking and launched a search."

Translation: *Vaughn* started panicking, not Reece. He always assigned his emotions to one of their other brothers, especially if he thought said emotions were not befitting of a former SEAL. Like panic, for instance.

"Hey, now." Eva stepped forward, putting herself between them. She didn't let go of Cam, though. Mainly because she'd probably topple over if she did. Hell, *he'd* probably topple over if she did.

"Don't be mad at him. He was commiser...acating with me over my horrible taste in men." She pouted and tipped her head back to gaze up at Cam. "Why the does everyone lie to me?"

"Commiserating?" Vaughn sneered. "Is that what you call getting him shitfaced drunk?"

"Vaughn..." Cam said with a note of warning that clearly told his twin to back the fuck off the protective "big" brother routine. The guy was only ten minutes older for christssakes.

He turned his attention back to Eva and gave her a light squeeze. "I've never lied to you."

Well, not exactly. Some might call him keeping his feelings to himself a lie, but he preferred to think of it as an omission for her own good. If he told her how he felt, she might get her hopes up, start fantasizing about that happily ever after she secretly craved, and he wasn't the kind of man that could give it. He was not the marriage or family type and he couldn't hurt her like that.

But he'd *never* tell her an outright lie.

"That's because you're a good friend." She patted his chest and looked at Vaughn, her chin lifting in defense. "And he's not drunk."

Vaughn glared at them both. "Bullshit. He can't even stand up straight."

"Okay, maybe I am," Cam said. "What's it to you? I don't need your permission to have a few."

Vaughn growled low in his throat, his bad mood darkening the air around him like a cloud. And what the fuck was up with that? While he definitely wasn't always roses and sunshine, he wasn't usually a flat-out jerk like this, either.

"Man, who stuck a poker up your ass and left it there? C'mon, leave Eva alone. She's already had a rough night."

"No, it's fine, Cam. Although…" She gave Vaughn an apprising up-down that would have scalded a lesser man. "It still astounds me that you two share the same DNA when he's a complete jackass and you're…well, not. All the time."

Vaughn's lip curled. "He got all the good genes."

"Obviously. Now if you'll excuse us, I need to go to my room before I pass out, and Cam is the only thing holding me up right now. So, shoo, evil twin."

Cam tried not to laugh. He really did, but Vaughn looked like one of those angry Saturday morning cartoon characters, the ones with heaving chests and bulging eyes and smoke pouring out of their ears. Besides, Cam was usually the first to defend his twin, but this time, Vaughn deserved to be knocked down a peg. Whatever had put him in such a pissy mood, he didn't need to be taking it out on Eva.

Without another word, Vaughn stalked past them, heading toward the bar they'd just left.

"I recommend the Prairie Fire," Eva called after him.

Cam grinned and jabbed the button for the elevator, which had left without them. "He'll probably like it. His SEAL buddies call him Tabasco because he carries around a plastic bottle of the stuff and puts it on everything."

Eva made a face. "Really? Gross."

"Yup. We may share our DNA, but we definitely weren't born with the same taste buds."

The elevator arrived and they stepped inside. The ride up to the fourth floor started in an easy silence, but the confined space and the way she leaned against his side, her breast occasionally brushing his arm, started to get to him. He caught a light floral scent from her hair and he dipped his head closer to breathe it in. Probably just her shampoo since he knew for a fact she rarely wore perfume. Even so, he found the scent intoxicating.

Or maybe that was just the alcohol in his system.

Or a mixture of both.

A distant, muffled alarm started signaling in the back of his mind as the elevator opened to their floor. Her room was only three doors to the left. His and Vaughn's was six doors to the right, and part of him—the part shooting off warning flares—thought this should be his stop. He could stand right here by the elevator and watch her until she was safely inside her room. Then he'd go back downstairs and—

"Would you mind staying with me for a while?" she blurted, then glanced away. "I'm, uh, not really ready to be alone with my thoughts yet."

Bad. Idea.

Very. Bad. Idea.

He completely ignored the warning klaxon now blaring in his head. In that moment, with the alcohol a pleasant hum in his brain and her standing there in that red dress looking both disheveled and sexy, he would have done anything for her.

"Absolutely."

Chapter Five

Eva fumbled her key before getting it into the slot and shoving down the handle to open her room's door. She weaved inside and found a light switch that turned on the bedside lamp. But the light made her feel self-conscious and she wasn't quite sure what to do with herself as she faced Cam. He'd paused at the threshold, his hand on the door jamb for support. His gaze swept over the room, taking in the rattan furniture and the windows that offered a 180 degree view of the ocean. Then his eyes locked on the king-sized bed.

Her stomach did a funny flurry thing as she set her key card on top of the mini-fridge positioned in a nook between the bathroom and the main part of the room. She opened the fridge and grabbed two of the hotel's ridiculously priced bottles of water. "We should probably have some water or we're gonna hate ourselves tomorrow. We can sit out on the balcony and…talk. Or something. Whatever."

Cam hadn't set foot in the room and his gaze was still fastened on the bed. She wasn't sure if he'd even heard her rambling.

"Cam?"

His throat worked, and he closed his eyes for a moment as if in pain. "You know, I should go. I have…" He waved a hand in a vague motion behind him.

"Oh. Of course. It's your brother's wedding. I'm sorry. Don't worry, I'm fine now."

"No, it's not—" He met her gaze for a bare instant, only long enough for her to notice the heat in his eyes. He cursed, and his voice came out thick. "I should just…go."

"Okay."

He hesitated, then stepped back. "See ya," he said before the door fell shut.

"Yeah." Her shoulders sagged under the brutal weight of disappointment. "See ya, Cam."

She stood rooted to the spot for a long time, until she realized tears had blurred her vision.

Dammit, she'd just taken an all-expenses paid trip to self-pity land, which included such fun rides as the self-doubt roller coaster and the insecurity-inducing house of mirrors.

"Ugh." She swiped a hand over her eyes. "Pull up your big girl panties now, Eva."

She returned the water to the fridge then forced herself to move, but only made it as far as the end of the bed. She sank to the plush mattress and stared at her bare toes with the fuck-me-now red pedicure her sister had insisted on before she left D.C.

After a few minutes, the quiet in the room began to press her down, made it hard to breathe.

Oh, God, she had wanted Cam to stay. Wanted to feel his hands on her again, his mouth against hers. She'd wanted... things that she shouldn't want in conjunction with him. Most of all, she'd wanted him to make her forget everything, which wasn't fair for so many reasons. Besides, she'd already monopolized most of his evening when he had family obligations.

And even telling herself all that, it hurt like hell that he'd walked away.

As her eyes began to tear up again, she dove for the TV remote and switched on the set. The local news came on, and she flipped through until she found an all-music channel playing country. She turned the volume down until Lady Antebellum's *Need You Now* was little more than white noise in the background.

Okay, this wasn't so bad. Now that she didn't have to listen to herself think, she could handle this. She needed to deal with the alcohol in her system or she'd wake up with a killer hangover. No problem. She'd draw a bath in the Jacuzzi tub, gulp down some Tylenol and a few bottles of water, then just enjoy a relaxing night. By herself. Because Preston sure as hell hadn't wanted her. And Cam—

Well, it was better that he didn't want her like that, right? She bombed at the whole dating thing, and how many times had Cam told her he wasn't looking for a committed relationship? Sex with him would only end in disaster, and she didn't want to lose the only solid, stable thing she had in her life. So, yes, it was a good thing he didn't want her. It was.

Now if she could just convince her libido of that.

Exasperated with herself, she stood and reached under her skirt to finally yank off the damn thong.

Ah. So much better.

She wadded the horrible excuse for underwear and shot it toward the garbage can, but a sharp rap on the door made her jump and threw off her aim. The thong landed artfully on the desk lamp.

Who the hell…?

She reached through the slit in her dress and rested her hand on her gun. She'd felt naked without it so, much to her sister's dismay, she'd made sure the dress would hide a slim thigh holster. Thank God. Unexpected knocks on hotel room doors usually didn't end well.

She peeked through the peep hole.

Cam.

Relaxing, she opened the door. "Hey, you scared the shit outta me. What—"

He didn't let her finish. He stepped toward her, cupped a hand around the back of her neck, and pulled her lips to his, swallowing her gasp of surprise. His mouth tasted of minty toothpaste, and his hair was soaked, the spiky dark strands dripping down his back and shoulders as if he hadn't bothered to dry off after a shower. He still wore the outrageous Hawaiian shirt, but it was unbuttoned, thrown back on as an afterthought. His shorts hung low, highlighting the V of muscle at his hips and doing little to conceal how very aroused he was.

She should push him away. Hadn't she already decided this couldn't happen between them? It was only going to complicate things and—

He flattened his free hand across the small of her back, drawing her flush against him, and his erection thrust insistently at her belly.

"Oh…" Everything female in her shuddered with pleasure and her mind blanked of all but his taste, his scent, and a rising tide of anticipation. All such a delicious reprieve from the emotional turbulence of the evening, and she let herself melt into his kiss. Her nipples hardened under the silky material of her dress as she rubbed against his hard body. He maneuvered them far enough into the room that he was able to kick the door shut, then spun and pressed her back against the cool metal. His hands roamed under the skirt of her dress, found her ass, and boosted her up. She locked her legs around his hips. He was giving her the gift of release and, dammit, she needed it. Needed *him*. Right here, right now.

"Tell me to stop," he groaned even as he surged hard against her, hitting all the right spots despite the maddening layer of his shorts still between them.

Eva dug her fingers into his scalp and gave his hair a punishing tug. "Don't you dare."

Her words vibrated through him, left him shaking with need.

He'd tried to do the right thing and walk away. He'd gone to his room with the intention of taking some time to sober up before heading back to the reception. Brushed his teeth on autopilot, then jumped under the cold spray of a shower, which did nothing to cool him down. He'd taken himself in hand to deal with his insistent boner—and then he'd stopped.

What the fuck was he doing, being all noble and shit,

when he knew she wanted him as much as he wanted her? If she had invited him in for a simple, friendly chat, she would have been calm, not fidgeting.

She wanted it. And damn the consequences, so did he.

He pinned her to the door with his hips, grinding against her. She went wild in his arms, her hands tracing his back and shoulders, her lips devouring his as she met his every thrust. Like trying to harness a tornado.

He shifted, letting his left arm take her weight, and stepped back just enough to drop a hand between their bodies. He found her wet and ready against his fly. No panties.

For the love of…

Had she been bare under that flowing red skirt all night?

The idea drove him almost past the point of civilized thought.

He played his fingers over her entrance, enjoying her quick intake of breath when he dipped into her in a sneak preview of what was to come. She was hot and tight, her muscles clenching on his fingers like she wanted to keep what he was giving her and take even more. She threw her head back against the door and groaned his name.

His name.

A roar of triumph filled his head. Maybe it even rumbled from his throat. He didn't give a damn. Eva was calling his name. Finally.

Christ, he had to be inside her.

He freed himself from his shorts, caught her hips under the skirt of her dress, and lifted her onto him. She arched and accepted him deep inside with a low moan.

Hot, slick, and so soft.

Cam lifted his gaze to make sure she really was Eva

and not a dream version, because "soft" was never a word he'd associated with her before this moment. Her body was long, lean muscle. Her spirit all passionate stubbornness and strength—

But then her silken walls tightened around his cock and, fuck yeah, there was the strength he adored about her. Perfect. She felt just as good as he always imagined she would, and he closed his eyes with the pleasure of it.

She writhed against him, her heels digging into his ass. "Oh. Oh, God. Move!"

"No." He pinned her to the door with his hips and caught her wrists in one hand, stretching her arms up over her head. She had her eyes squeezed tight, and he leaned in to brush his mouth over her lids. "Look at me."

Her eyes opened. "Move. Please."

"No."

With a frustrated cry, she arched her back as much as she was able, pinned to the door as she was, and the movement rippled her inner muscles, squeezing them hard around his cock again. Heat gathered in his lower back. Oh, too close. They were both too close and he wasn't ready for that yet. His balls tightened, and he clenched his teeth against the urge to pound into her, despite the beads of sweat sliding down his spine from the effort of restraint. He'd waited too damn long for this to lose all control now and have it be over in mere seconds.

"Dammit," she gasped. "I need you to move."

Her trapped fingers flexed as if she wanted to touch him, run her fingers through his hair, dig her nails into his shoulders. He shuddered at the mental image, but didn't release her hands. Next time. This round, he was calling all the shots.

Curling his hips the tiniest bit, he found her ear with his teeth. "Say my name again, Eva."

"No."

"Stubborn." He reached between them and found her clit, gave it a teasing rub and watched her eyes all but roll back in her head. She whimpered when he withdrew the pressure, a sound she would no doubt hate herself for later, but that he found insanely sexy.

"My name."

A small smile flitted over her lips as she shook her head. Her dark hair, smelling of sun and saltwater and her floral shampoo, swept his shoulder with the gesture. Fuck, she'd turned the tables, now teasing him as much as he was her. And, somehow, he was losing this little match of wills.

Unable to stay still any longer, he rolled his hips and her body opened wider to him, accepting more of him with each languorous thrust. It still wasn't enough for her. She dug her heels into his back, demanding more. Demanding hard, fast, and dirty. And he'd give her all that — as soon as he got what he wanted. He wound the strands of her hair around his hand and tugged, exposing her neck to his mouth.

"Say my name."

She groaned. "Uh-uh."

"Who is inside you, Eva?" He punctuated each word with a shallow thrust. "Tell me who is fucking you."

She squirmed and tried to pull her hands free from his grip. "Cam."

Yes. A primal satisfaction short-circuited his brain. He released her hands and her nails instantly bit into his scalp. Grasping her hips, he pumped into her, each thrust pushing her higher and knocking their bodies against the door.

"Say it again."

"Camden," she whispered and dragged his mouth to hers. She caught his lower lip between her teeth and tugged, and his control evaporated. Supporting her weight with his hands under her ass, he spun away from the door and strode toward the king sized bed. Her head fell back as each step pushed him deeper inside her, and he couldn't resist the tantalizing view of her cleavage. He dipped his head to taste the hollow between her breasts that the damn dress had been giving him teasing glimpses of all night long—and he lost his balance, snagging his foot on some kind of strap. Eva squealed as they toppled to the bed, and he twisted so that he took the brunt of the fall on his back, Eva on top of him.

Straddling his hips, she grinned down at him. "You're such a klutz." She dragged her palms over his bare chest, stopping only to pinch his nipples lightly between her fingers. "Hmm. But I do like this view."

"Not tonight." He easily flipped her to her back and silenced her indignant cry with a hard kiss. "Next time. I've waited too long to have you under me."

He plucked at the tie holding the halter dress up and about swallowed his tongue when the red fabric fell free. He'd spent many nights fantasizing about seeing her naked and now…

Damn. Fantasy didn't even come close.

She had small, firm breasts with dusky pink nipples standing at taut peaks. He sucked one into his mouth, giving it all his attention for a long moment before moving to the other one. As he sucked her, he stripped the dress off her legs and she lay before him in nothing but a thigh holster and her favorite Glock.

Holy fuck, that was hot. So, so much better than fantasy.

Eva lifted her arms over her head and arched her back, her silky, flat belly teasing his cock as she hooked a leg around his hip. "Why are you not naked yet?"

In a surge, she sat up and shoved his unbuttoned shirt off his shoulders, then pushed his shorts down his hips. He had to leave her and stand long enough to kick off the shorts. They landed with a dull *whop* somewhere over by the door, but he didn't care. He edged Eva's thighs apart with his knee, took another second to remove her gun and holster and set them aside, then lifted her hips in his hands. He entered her slowly, watching himself sink into her.

Beautiful. Every inch of her. And watching her accept him into her body…

His. She was his.

He lost it. Still kneeling between her legs, he hammered into her and lifted her hips to meet each plunge. He hooked her legs over his shoulders and watched her breasts bounce as he went to town. The bed springs creaked, and the headboard banged against the wall until Eva grabbed the edge to steady herself.

"Cam," she gasped.

"Yes. Keep saying my name. I want it on your lips when you come."

Oh, it was on her lips all right. She ignited a second later, screaming his name, when he pressed his thumb to her clit. It was all he needed. He pumped his hips once, twice more, then found his own release in hard jets that left him shaking.

"Holy shit." Eva's legs dropped off his shoulders and thunked heavily to the mattress. "We should've done this a long time ago."

Cam collapsed forward, catching himself on his hands on either side of her head, and balanced over her for a long time. Waited for his breathing to settle. "We're gonna do it again real soon."

She snorted. "I can't move."

That hollow where her shoulder met her neck was intriguing. He lowered himself on top of her, careful to balance most of his weight on his forearms, and traced the spot with his lips. She made a cute little sound somewhere between a gasp and a moan. He smiled against her skin and tested the area with his tongue. She squirmed. Yup. They were going to do it again sooner than she thought, and he was going to take his time with round two. Now that he'd gotten years of pent up sexual tension out of his system, he could slow it down.

Tease.

Explore.

Before the night was over, he planned to know every square inch of Eva Cardoso's body by heart.

Chapter Six

As the first tendrils of pink lit the sky in the east, the slight change from complete dark to half-dark roused Eva from a doze and her stomach lurched. Overhead, the ceiling started a slow spin.

Oh, God. She was going to be sick.

She bolted toward the bathroom. Since all of her friends were men who knew how to pack away alcohol, she'd built up a decent tolerance over the years and hadn't prayed to the porcelain god since college. She made up for lost time now, retching until she had nothing left in her stomach. Drinking all those shots in quick succession had been such a bad idea.

Eva flushed the toilet and brushed her teeth, then glugged some mouthwash directly out of the tiny complimentary bottle. But, no. The alcoholic burn made her stomach threaten another revolt. She gagged and spit it out.

Straightening, she surveyed her naked reflection in the mirror. Her hair stuck up around her head in a knotted mess.

Her nipples puckered in the air-conditioned chill, and a vivid memory of a hot mouth teasing them had her dampening expectantly in the tender place between her thighs.

Sex hair. Swollen lips. Chin and cheeks chaffed by beard stubble. Happy nipples. She looked like a well-loved woman. So why did she feel so hollow?

Tell me to stop.

Oh, no. No, no, no.

With her head completely clear for the first time in hours, she staggered from the bathroom. No way did she have wild against-the-door sex with Cam. In the midst of her alcoholic daze, she must have superimposed his face over some other guy's. She'd done it at least once before—okay, more than once. In fact, more often than she cared to admit, she'd let her imagination wander to him while she was in bed with Preston. But it wasn't being unfaithful. Sometimes she needed a little extra something to reach orgasm, and the forbidden fruit fantasy was her favorite.

Fantasy being the key word.

Please, not Cam. She'd be okay seeing anybody else in that bed except him. He was the only steady, uncomplicated thing in her life, and if she'd gone and fucked it all up—well, then she was no better than her mother.

Eva stumbled to a halt and wrapped her arms around her middle, gulping down another surge of sickness. In her absence, Cam—it was definitely him—had sprawled in the most awkward position, his arms wrapped around two pillows, one leg bent slightly at the knee, the other extended with his foot hanging off the edge of the mattress, and his body twisted so he was half on his stomach and half on his side.

He was naked.

From the foot of the bed, she had a perfect view of all his assets. Wide shoulders. Tribal tattoo wrapping his right shoulder and bicep. A slim waist and the sexy as hell dip at the small of his back dusted lightly with hair. A tight, muscular ass. Thick thighs.

And…everything else.

Semi-erect, his cock pressed into the mattress. His hips even moved in his sleep as if he dreamed of taking her again.

He had taken her, too. Completely. He'd dominated her and she'd let him. Worse, she enjoyed it. She'd never before allowed her lovers to take absolute control like that. So why had she let Cam?

Holy shit. She'd slept with Cam.

What had she done?

Panic kicked her heart rate into a gallop, and she couldn't draw a full breath. She couldn't face him in the light of day. What would she say? Thanks? And what about their friendship? Would he wake up expecting more than that from her?

I've waited too long to have you under me.

Oh, she couldn't do this.

Frantic to escape, she gathered her bathroom things as quietly as possible. She'd already repacked her clothes in anticipation of her departure tomorrow morning, and her bag still lay on the floor, right where Cam had tripped over it. Her dress spilled off the corner of the bed and pooled to the floor like a splash of satin blood. She didn't bother putting it back on, but stuffed it in her bag and found a pair of cotton shorts, a support tank, and a comfy over-sized T-shirt. Nor did she bother with a brush, opting instead to tie her hair up in a sloppy bun. She grabbed her gun and holster from the bedside table. A pair of flip-flops, her key card, and she was out the door with her bag slung over her shoulder.

She needed space. And time. And to be completely sober. Maybe then she'd be capable of processing this one night stand like a mature, rational adult.

Because right now, she sure as fuck didn't feel the least bit rational.

Sunlight splashed over the bed, warm and cheery—and completely fucking merciless in its brightness. It stabbed through Cam's eyelids like two flaming stakes, jolting him from a dead sleep. Groaning, he stuffed his head under a pillow with every intention of going back to dreamland until his brain stopped pounding. But now that he was semiconscious, he couldn't shake the niggling sense that something was…off. He eased the pillow away from his face and blinked a couple times at the light. What brilliant designer decided it was a good idea to line two of the four walls in the room with floor-to-ceiling windows anyway? Especially when one such wall faced directly east. Were people not allowed to sleep past dawn in Key West?

Okay, so it wasn't exactly dawn. The alarm clock on the bedside table said it was a little after ten. But anything before noon was ungodly early after a night like last night.

Although, in truth, he didn't feel half bad. Besides the expected hangover headache and some tightness in his lower back, he was pretty damn happy. He lay sprawled across the bed on his belly, the sheet in a twisted knot around his legs and hips. All of the pillows scattered the floor, save for the one he'd burrowed underneath when the blasted sunshine woke him—

Wait. The other half of the bed was empty.

Eva.

Cam bolted upright and hissed as his head made it known in no uncertain terms that it despised him at the moment. He disengaged his legs from the sheet and sat up on the edge of the mattress, cradling his forehead in his palms until some of the throbbing subsided. After several long minutes, he cautiously lifted his gaze to scan the room.

Her dress was gone. So was the duffel bag that he'd tripped over the night before.

"No." He scrambled to his feet, crossed the room, and pulled open the closet, a small part of him hoping maybe she'd stashed the bag out of the way before a morning coffee run.

Nope. Empty.

Bathroom, too.

The only thing she'd left behind was a thong hanging from the desk lamp.

"Goddammit!" Anger mixed liberally with despair into a nasty slurry in his stomach. He shoved the closet door shut hard enough to rattle it in its frame, than banged the flat of his hand against it because slamming it hadn't been satisfying enough.

She'd up and left without waking him or leaving a note. And he bet when he got back to his room and checked his phone, there would be no call or text from her, either. She might as well have shoved a knife in his back before she took off. Would have hurt a helluva lot less.

The locking mechanism on the front door whirred and

Cam spun toward it, his heart doing a fleetingly hopeful jig behind his ribs. So maybe Eva *had* gone out for coffee or—

The door swung open. And while the maid standing on the other side shared Eva's caramel complexion and dark hair, coloring was the only resemblance between them. Small and curvy, the maid had a weathered, *been there, done that* look to her and she wore her graying hair in a tail tight enough to give her an automatic face-lift. She froze when she spotted him, the master key card dropping from her hand. It was on one of those retractable chains and whipped back to the clip on her apron with a *ziiip* sound that was unnaturally loud in the awkward silence.

And there he stood, his tackle on display for anyone walking by in the hallway. "Uh…"

The maid crossed her arms underneath her ample breasts. "You need to leave," she said in a heavy smoker's voice with only the slightest hint of a Spanish accent. After the initial shock of seeing him wore off, she didn't seem the least bit fazed by his nudity, but he still snapped up his shorts from where they'd dropped last night and tugged them on.

"The woman staying in this room…do you know where she is?" he asked as he bent to retrieve his shirt.

Her disapproving frown only deepened. "Not here. She checked out this morning. Now you need to leave or I'll call security."

And there went his last shred of hope that last night had meant more to Eva than a wham, bam, thank you, sir.

Cam breathed out in a soft sigh of resignation then fished his own key card out of his pocket. He held it up between two fingers and showed it to the maid. "No, don't do that. I'm a guest here, too."

"Not in this room you're not."

"No, I'm not," he agreed and shot one last glance at the bed. "I'm leaving."

Vaughn wasn't in their room when Cam got there, which he counted as a blessing. Boiling for a fight, he wasn't fit for public consumption at the moment, and it wouldn't have been fair to take all of his frustration out on his twin. He stripped as soon as the door clicked shut behind him and gave serious consideration to tossing his clothes in the trash. He could smell Eva and sex on them, and he wanted no reminder. But in the end, he folded them into his suitcase, then headed for the bathroom to start the shower.

The near-scalding water cleaned away the blackest part of his mood. He even felt marginally human again when he stepped out. By the time he dried off and dressed in a fresh T-shirt and his favorite pair of blue jeans, his headache had dulled and his stomach had settled enough that food sounded like a good idea. Preferably something greasy and artery clogging.

He grabbed his key card from the dresser and made his way down to the restaurant attached to the hotel's lobby, all the while hoping he didn't run into the maid again. Nothing like having a witness to your morning after walk of shame.

At the restaurant, he found Vaughn sitting in a corner booth with his SEAL buddies, Gabe and Quinn. None of them had much left on their plates, so they'd been there for a while already.

"Hey," Gabe said when he joined them. "Thanks for your help last night with Seth."

"Huh? Oh. Yeah." Cam waved a hand and took the empty spot on the bench seat next to his twin. With everything else, he'd almost forgotten about that whole incident. "I didn't do anything but talk to him."

"At least he'll talk to you," Quinn said. "He shuts down around us."

The scent of food made Cam's stomach howl, but the waiter was nowhere to be seen. He reached over and stole a slice of bacon off Vaughn's plate. "Well, you guys are technically Seth's bosses. He's not gonna want to air his dirty laundry in front of you. Does he have anyone else to talk to? A peer?"

Gabe and Quinn looked at each other, then Quinn shrugged. "The other guys on the team...they haven't quite accepted him yet."

"He's being diplomatic. They don't want him," Gabe said in his typical blunt way. "They think he's dangerous. Frankly, so do I."

Yeah, that was an argument Cam wasn't about to get in the middle of. And yet, he couldn't stand the thought of Seth having nobody neutral to talk to on the team. "If he ever needs to talk, send him my way, okay? Jude has my number."

"Thanks," Quinn said.

From there, the conversation veered into lighter topics until the waiter finally showed. Cam ordered a double stack of pancakes, bacon, and some black coffee. The two former SEALs settled their bills and stood to leave, but Gabe paused and turned back to the table.

"Cam, you were Air Force, weren't you?"

He lifted his coffee in a salute. "Four years, Security Forces."

"Know of any pilots looking for work in the private sector?"

"Why, you hiring?"

Gabe nodded. "We need one before we take on anything

more serious than bodyguard jobs."

Cam thought about it, running through a mental list of his pilot friends. Most wouldn't qualify for the kind of mercenary work Gabe dealt in, being either married with families or in stable careers as commercial airline pilots—except for Jace Garcia. The guy was a hothead, known for charging into situations like a bull, earning him the nickname Toro. He was smart, capable, and a bit crazy. Come to think of it, he'd probably fit in well with Gabe's team. "There's only one guy I can think of right now. Last I talked to him, he was flying corporate big wigs around Texas and hating every minute of it. I'll give him a call, gauge his interest. Is there a way he can get in touch with you?"

Gabe produced a business card and handed it over, then after a round of goodbyes, the SEALs left.

Vaughn waited all of a half second before nailing Cam with a look that said, *all right, spill it,* and his hackles rose.

"What?"

"Where were you all night?"

Cam's jaw locked. "You know damn well," he said through his teeth.

"Yeah, that's what I thought. That was a huge mistake, bro."

"I kinda figured that out when I woke up and found her gone."

Vaughn shook his head and picked up his coffee. "Now what are you gonna do?"

"Can't do anything till we get home."

"And then?" Vaughn prompted.

He shrugged, pretending all kinds of nonchalance that he didn't feel. "Then…I don't know."

Chapter Seven

Cam turned up his collar against the icy November wind chasing dead leaves across the pavement and fought down a surge of envy as he waited for his informant to show. Jude and Libby had stayed in Key West for their honeymoon and were probably sitting together on the beach right this very minute, being all lovey-dovey with each other as they soaked in the beautiful weather.

Three days home, and Cam would give anything to see the sun again. Winter had arrived early and brutally, pounding the east coast with ice and snow storms and shutting down several major cities in the process. Luckily, D.C. had avoided the worst of it, but the weather forecasters were not optimistic about that trend continuing and gleefully spoke of an impending Snow-pocalypse.

He just hoped to be cozy at home before that happened.

Cam glanced up and down the quiet street dotted with abandoned warehouses and boarded up buildings. This part of the city was dying, struggling for every breath, but cities needed places like this. In a few years, some politician would probably see the potential charm and get it in mind to clean up these streets and revamp the warehouses into condos for yuppies, leaving the homeless squatters like his informant, Soup, without a roof over their heads once again.

Man, he wished he could get Soup some help, but if there was one thing he learned in his nine years on the force, you can't help those that don't want it. Soup was perfectly happy with his lot in life. Then again, Soup had all but pickled his brain and ruined a good career in banking with drugs and alcohol, so maybe he wasn't the best judge of what was good for him.

Happiness was relative anyway.

Look at him, for example. He had a roof over his head, clothes on his back, food to eat, and a decent job that made him a comfortable living, and he was wallowing in misery.

Three days home, and not a word from Eva. After several texts and the once-a-day messages he'd left on her voice mail had gone unanswered, he was starting to wonder if he'd ever hear from her again. Maybe he could drive by her place again when he left here —

No, that was a little too stalker-ish for comfort. He'd already spent way more time thinking about her than was probably healthy. Which, really, was par for the course. Sometime early in their partnership, his affection for Eva had blossomed into something much more dangerous, something he absolutely shouldn't have felt.

Love. He was completely, head-over-ass in love with her.

He couldn't pinpoint the exact moment it happened. It was more like a bunch of little moments that added up over the years, like that time she got so excited at a Redskins game she accidentally dumped her beer over his head. Or the first time she kicked his ass in a sparring match, then spent the rest of the day gloating about it. Her watery smile after that asshole Preston stood her up when she had tickets to a Blake Shelton concert, and Cam had arrived decked out in a cowboy hat and boots to take her, even though he hated country music. Or all the late nights at work, when they were so exhausted they were running on caffeine and fumes, and they'd burst into hysterical laughter over something as juvenile as the squeak of a chair sounding like a fart. Each of those moments had chipped away at his heart, bit by tiny bit, until she held the whole damn thing in her hands.

He'd spent the past five years being so careful not to jeopardize their relationship, but now he'd gone and fucked everything up for one drunken night of sex. He'd be lucky if she ever talked to him again.

Cursing under his breath, Cam studied the street again, desperate for a distraction from his current train of thought. Still empty. Where was Soup? After all the panicked messages the guy had left him while he was gone, you'd think he'd be on time.

Five more minutes, Cam decided, then he was out. He had better things to do than stand here, stiffening up in the wind.

The five minutes came and went.

"And that's a wrap." He turned to trudge back to his 4Runner and that's when he finally spotted Soup peeking around the corner of the nearest building.

"About fucking time," Cam said.

"Bad, bad news," Soup replied. He had a persistent twitch, a simultaneous jerk of his oily head and fast blink, and it got worse when he was upset or in withdrawal. Since he had a very fresh set of tracks up both of his bare arms, Cam assumed the twitch was from nerves.

"What bad news?"

"S-S-Someone…" Teeth chattering, he wrapped his arms around himself, which was going to do a whole helluva lot of nothing to fend off the chill since he wore only a ratty T-shirt.

Cam sighed, slipped off his coat, and draped it over his informant's shoulders. "Take this."

Soup huddled into it gratefully. "I-I-I always like you, Detective. G-g-good man. Good friend."

There was that *friend* word again. "Yeah, so I've been told." He straightened the collar, then zipped it up around the guy's skinny frame. "Keep this one this time, okay? No trading it for dope. I'm running out of jackets."

Soup nodded, twitched, and snuggled deeper into the flannel lining. After a moment, his shivers subsided.

"All right," Cam said, ignoring the wind that had gone from brutal to flaying without the protection of his coat. "Give me the bad news."

"Someone's asking around about you, man."

"Who?"

Soup lifted his shoulders in shrug. "Some white dude. Mean. Nice clothes."

Okay, then. That narrowed it down. He tried a new tactic. "What's the guy asking?"

"He asked me to kill ya for money."

Cam backed up a step, unsnapped the strap holding

his gun in his shoulder holster, and drew the weapon in a smooth, practiced move. "Back the fuck up. Now."

Outrage rippled over Soup's weathered face, but he held up his hands and backed up until he stood against the brick wall of a warehouse. "You think I'd do you like that, man?"

"I think you'll do just about anything for your next hit."

"Not that." Genuine hurt flickered through his glazed eyes. "I ain't no killer, man. You're my friend. That's why I tell you."

"All right," Cam said, but wasn't ready to lower his weapon just yet. "If you're a friend, you'll get me more info if he shows again, right? A name would be useful. A description of what he looks like and what he drives. How much he's asking."

"I can answer that!" Soup said and twitched in excitement. "A thousand big ones."

That's it? Wasn't his life worth a bit more than—

Cam gave himself a mental shake. It didn't matter. Yeah, a thousand wasn't a lot in the hired killer business, but to a guy in Soup's position, it might as well be a million. "Did he give you a reason why he wants me dead?"

"Said you did him wrong. I didn't axe no more questions after that."

"Well, I want you to 'axe' more questions," Cam said. "Talk to people, see who else he approached."

"Ah, man…"

"And you'll let me know the second he convinces someone to do the hit."

Soup shifted on his feet, gaze darting around the empty street like he expected a SWAT team to rush out of one of the buildings. Ignoring the gun, he sidled a step closer, and even in the cold and the wind, his body odor was amazing. He lowered his voice to a conspiratorial whisper. "Gonna cost more."

Yeah, what a pal. "Of course it is."

"Guy's gotta eat."

"Twenty now. Twenty for every additional *relevant* piece of info about this man." Cam finally lowered his gun, but didn't feel confident enough in Soup's intentions to holster it. One-handed, he slid two tens from his pocket. Soup tried to snatch them with scarred, dirty hands, but he pulled the cash out of reach. "No dope. You buy dope with this, I *will* know. It'll be the last payment you ever see from me. Deal?"

In full sulk mode, Soup mumbled something under his breath.

"Deal?" Cam said again.

"Yes," Soup said, louder.

"You know I'm not fucking around about the dope."

He nodded, eyes wide. "You see everything."

"Damn right I do." Cam finally relinquished the cash and watched as Soup squirreled it away into a pocket before scampering off.

Even though Cam was no longer on the force, he still had his finger on the pulse of this city, and it didn't hurt to remind the natives of that once in a while.

With the wind slicing through his long-sleeve T-shirt like a saw, he sprinted back to his SUV, parked out of sight a block away, and cranked up the heat as soon as the engine purred to life. He held his stiff fingers over the vent until the air started to blow hot and he could feel his extremities again, then found his phone charging on the dash where he left it and dialed his twin. As much as he'd rather not mention this conversation to anybody, Vaughn had to know about the hit because a drug addict looking to make a quick buck might not be able to differentiate between them.

"Hey," he said when Vaughn picked up. "You home?"

"Office," Vaughn answered.

"Stick around. I'll be there in fifteen. We have a situation."

The Wilde Security office sat in a rundown strip mall that was otherwise hopelessly vacant. Reece had bought the graffiti-covered building cheap and had set up shop in one of the seven empty stores with plans to restore the remaining six into office spaces they could rent out for extra income. But while it was a good idea in theory, none of the Wilde brothers knew the first thing about restoration, and most of the building was still boarded-up. The only cosmetic changes they'd accomplished so far were the darkly tinted front windows and the neat, white lettering that spelled out "Wilde Security" on the glass.

At least the neighborhood wasn't half bad anymore. It had experienced a revival over the past several years as young professionals flooded the area looking for cheaper rent, which in turn, had driven up housing costs and chased most of the gangbangers farther east. All of the graffiti was old, faded, and starting to chip and gave the building the look of an eighty-year-old with regrettable tattoos.

Cam guided his 4Runner into the parking lot, which had been freshly paved during the summer and glowed like an oil spill in the yellow splash of the street lamps. He parked next to Vaughn's Hummer, somewhat dismayed to also see Reece's new Scion FR-S and the ten-year-old Jeep Cherokee Greer drove when it was too cold for his Harley.

Damn. He'd really hoped only his twin was burning the midnight oil at the office tonight. Should have known better. Since they'd all been in Key West for the past week, things had piled up. Now, with Jude on his honeymoon, they were a man short and playing catch-up. To top it off, a new missing person case had come in this morning, which had fallen to Vaughn, who had an uncanny ability to track people.

No doubt, Vaughn was already on the trail, which explained why he was still at the office on a Friday night. Reece was always at the office because, workaholic that he was, he didn't have a social life outside of Wilde Security and his other business ventures. And if Greer had one, he didn't talk about it.

So, yeah, should have known they'd all be here.

Greer and Reece both had offices in the back of the building, while Cam shared the front area with Vaughn and Jude, so maybe he'd get lucky and his oldest brothers would be shut away doing expense reports or whatever they did. Then he could talk to his twin in private.

Or…not.

He pushed through the front door to find everyone gathered there, waiting. Figures. "Oh, lookie. A welcoming committee."

"What situation?" Greer demanded. "And where the hell is your coat?"

Cam barely suppressed the urge to roll his eyes. What was it about his oldest brother that made him feel like a teenager again? "Okay, *Dad*."

"Don't be an ass," Reece said. "That's Jude's job."

"Well, he's not here, so I guess I'll do the honors this week."

Reece shook his head. "Fucking younger brothers."

"Enough." Greer made a slicing motion through the air with the blade of his hand, effectively shutting everyone up. "Vaughn said you went out to meet an informant, and now you have a situation. What is it?"

Yeah, he wasn't so sure he wanted to share said situation with his brothers just yet. At least not until he had something more substantial than a drug addict's word. They'd blow the whole thing all out of proportion when it could be nothing. Hell, it probably was nothing. And even if it was something, he'd handle it. They didn't need to be involved.

"It's no big deal, guys. Really." He shrugged out of his shoulder holster, locking it and his firearm in the top drawer of his desk before grabbing the hoodie hanging from the back of his chair. He stuffed his arms in and zipped it half way, then faced his brothers again. "I just wanted to give Vaughn a heads up."

"About what?" Vaughn asked.

Cam met his gaze. As much as he'd rather skirt around the issue, it was pointless to keep evading because his twin could read him like a preschooler's alphabet book. It was only a matter of time until they all found out anyway. "Someone's been shopping around Soup's territory looking to put a hit out on me."

The room exploded with noise.

"What?" Reece said.

"You call that no big deal?" Greer asked.

Cam held his twin's gaze throughout, silently conveying how sorry he was for putting Vaughn in danger. *If* the threat was real, which he wasn't completely convinced of yet.

Vaughn inclined his head. He got the message and accepted it, which took a huge load off Cam's shoulders. Truthfully, he'd been more worried about Vaughn's reaction to the news than he was about the supposed hit.

"Who is it?" Greer asked, drawing him back into the conversation.

"Dunno yet. Working on it."

Greer nodded. "We're all going to work on it."

"No, don't." Sighing, he propped himself against the edge of his desk and rubbed his hands over his face. "C'mon, you know how many people I've had threaten me over the years? How many murderers I've put away that vow to take their revenge? This is probably nothing. I mean, who goes shopping for a hired killer among burnt out drug addicts?"

"He's got a point," Vaughn said.

"See? You guys have enough on your plates—Vaughn with his new case, and you two, keeping us flush with clients so we can pay our bills. And, Reece, don't you have another home security gig coming up? You don't have to drop everything. I'll handle this."

Greer punched him in the shoulder. Hard. "That's not how this family works, Cam, and you sure as hell know it. Someone fucks with one of us, they fuck with us all. Understood?"

Although Cam had been out of the military for nearly ten years, he still felt an urge to salute whenever Greer used his Army Ranger tone like that.

Instead, he punched Greer's shoulder back just as hard. "10-4, big bro. But at least give me time to verify the threat is valid, okay?"

His brothers looked at each other.

"And if it is real, you can throw me in a safe house somewhere." Not that he'd actually go, but if the little white lie got his brothers off the subject, he was a-okay with it. "Then you can drop everything and call in the freakin' National Guard to find the guy if you want."

The tension in the room broke with Greer's abrupt bark of laugher. "The National Guard couldn't find their asses with a GPS and an arrow pointing the way. You call in the Rangers if you want someone found."

"Excuse me?" Vaughn said, eyes narrowing. He crossed his arms over his chest. "You meant the SEALs, right?"

"Nah. You call the SEALs when you want someone killed. You call the Rangers when you want them found."

Vaughn clicked his tongue against his teeth. "We're gonna have to agree to disagree there, bro."

"What's there to disagree about?" Reece asked. He'd gone the intelligence route rather than into the Rangers like Greer, but he was no less loyal to Mother Army for it. "It's a straight-up fact."

"Oh, so it's two against one now? That's how it's gonna be?" Squaring off against the two of them, Vaughn crooked a finger. "Bring it, Army brats."

Cam slipped past them and made it to the parking lot before he let his grin loose. Need to escape an uncomfortable conversation with Greer and Reece? Bring up the National Guard and wait. The age-old branch rivalry would do the rest, especially when Vaughn was around to egg it on.

Cam opened the door of his 4Runner, heard something crash in the office, and laughed. Yup. Worked like a charm every time.

Chapter Eight

"Yo, Wilde!"

Eva's stomach hit the floor at Detective Miguel de la Rosa's shout from across the office. Oh, Christ, no. Please don't let it be Cam. It couldn't be him. He wasn't a morning person and had no reason to be at the police station this early. Maybe it was one of his brothers. Yes, that was possible. Reece and Greer both came by fairly regularly.

At the moment, she'd take any of the Wilde brothers but Cam. He'd called her several times in the four days since returning from Key West, and she'd agonized over her phone each time his name showed on the caller ID. She wanted to pick up and play it cool like their one night stand never happened, but whenever she worked up the nerve to answer, she'd remember his lips, hard on hers, kissing her senseless. His hands, pinning hers to the mattress. His voice, demanding that she say his name as she climaxed hard enough to see stars.

Dammit. His voice.

That *was* his voice answering Miguel with a, "Hey, long time."

She heard a clap of palms and looked up from her computer screen in time to see her old partner and her new partner pull each other in for one of those manly, backslapping hugs.

"You tired of playing Dick Tracey yet?" Miguel asked. "Ready to come back and do some real police work?"

"Nah, man. I kinda like the P.I. lifestyle. The work's mostly interesting. Plus, no mandatory overtime or holiday hours."

"Aw, fuck me," Miguel said.

"You're not really my type."

Yeah, because *she* was his type. Eva wanted to melt from embarrassment and sank down in her chair. She sensed his gaze traveling over her head.

"Eva still here?"

"She was… Oh. Huh," Miguel said. "I don't see her anymore. Probably went home. We worked the night shift."

Yes, she'd gone home. No Eva here. Now if only Cam would turn around and leave because she really couldn't face him. Not at work in front of everyone. Her reputation would never recover—and goddamn him, he *knew* that. He knew how hard she worked to be seen as another one of the guys.

How dare he put her in this position?

He wouldn't have had to if you answered his calls, a small voice of reason reminded her.

No. Fuck reason. Anger was so much easier than the other emotions his mere presence jumbled up inside her.

One night did not give him the right to stop by *her* place of employment and chat with *her* co-workers. So what if they used to be his, too. They weren't anymore, and he shouldn't be here, period.

Full of righteous indignation, she shot to her feet, intending to give him a piece of her mind. But then he spotted her, his dimple flashed in a smile, and butterflies rattled around in her belly.

He wore a new black nylon jacket instead of the beat to shit Carhartt that he'd had since she met him. The open zipper revealed a gray button-down that he wore as easily as he did a T-shirt. His dark-wash jeans looked crisp and new, and he'd combed his hair back from his face.

Had he dressed up for her?

Weird.

Too weird.

As was the fact that she no longer wanted to punch him. Actually, she found herself staring at his mouth and the insanely sexy dimple indenting his left cheek.

The man was fucking gorgeous. Why had she never noticed before?

He said a quick goodbye to Miguel and was half way across the office before she realized he'd moved.

Oh, shit.

She dropped into her chair and started gathering witness reports, desperately needing something to do as he drew even with her desk. He said nothing for a long moment, and her hands started to tremble. She hated being so nervous around him, but what exactly was she supposed to say to him now?

Like so many times before when they worked together,

he set a Kit Kat bar on the edge of her desk. "I tried calling. And texting. I, uh, actually stopped just short of stalking."

She accepted the candy peace offering with a half-smile pulling uncomfortably at her cheeks, and her hand lingered on his. She couldn't help herself. She wanted to feel skin-to-skin contact with him again, which was so fucking wrong on so many different levels.

She jerked away and covered the gaffe by tucking the candy into the top drawer of her desk. "I know."

"Yeah, figured as much." He stuffed his hands in the pockets of his jacket and gazed around at the overflowing desks jammed together in an office not quite big enough for all of them. Coffee scented the air, which hummed with constant activity from phones ringing and detectives talking. The place wasn't nicknamed the Hive for nothing.

"Hasn't changed much around here," Cam said.

Bull. It changed irrevocably the day he quit to join his brothers in starting up Wilde Security, but she couldn't tell him that now. There would be all kinds of sexual subtext in anything she said.

This sucked. Big time.

"Eva." He squatted down beside her desk until they were eye level. "Can we go somewhere, grab a bite to eat for breakfast, and figure this out?"

Yes, a part of her all but screamed with relief, but at the same time, another part recoiled at the idea of having such a heavy conversation with *Camden,* of all people. It just wasn't right. Couldn't they pretend nothing happened?

She opened her mouth to say something—she had no idea what—but Miguel sauntered up and saved her from having to figure it out.

"Looks like we're not going home yet," he said. "Call just came in."

Thank God. Murder, she could handle.

She stood so fast, Cam had to back up or risk getting hit in the face. "I have to go."

Cam straightened and blew out a breath. "Sure, but we do have to talk."

"Yeah, of course. We will." She grabbed Miguel by the sleeve of his shirt and tugged him away from her desk. And away from Cam.

"Saved by the murder, huh?" Miguel said once they were out of earshot. He glanced over his shoulder, but she continued tugging him forward, bypassing the elevator for the stairs.

"Shut up." She hit the push bar for the stairwell door and took the steps down in a jog.

He grinned and followed at an easier pace. "I'm detecting lots of interesting undercurrents between you two all of the sudden. Did you finally fuck?"

Eva whipped around. "What? No, of course not. He's my best friend, nothing more."

"Uh-huh." Miguel appeared thoroughly unconvinced.

"Oh, God." Defeat rolled through her and dragged her down to sit on one of the steps. "Does everyone know?"

"*Chica*," he said in the same admonishing tone she'd heard him use with his teenage granddaughters and ruffled her hair as he passed. "You work with a bunch of detectives. We've always known it was never a question of *if* with you two, but *when*." He stopped a few steps down and gazed back with a knowing expression. "So, was it Key West?"

She sighed. She didn't have to answer. He already knew.

The whole freaking department already knew.

"Hah!" He did a celebratory Ricky Ricardo dance move down the rest of the stairs. "I won the bet."

Whoa. Bet? That got her moving again. She chased him out into the parking lot. "Hold up, de la Rosa. You *bet* on my sex life?"

"Call it living vicariously."

"I'll call it illegal gambling," she told him and rounded the hood of her car.

"Aw, *chica*." Opening the passenger side door, he pouted at her over the roof. "Can't an old man have a little fun?"

"Not at my expense, okay?"

His brow furrowed. "Never. But I thought—" He looked back up at the stationhouse. "Shit, is there something wrong between you and Wilde?"

More than something. Everything. And she did not want to talk about it. She shook her head and slid in behind the wheel. "Where's this murder?"

Chapter Nine

Karma was a complete bitch.

Eva pulled her Taurus into her driveway and killed the engine, then took a moment to lay her head against the seat and breathe out. The scent of death and garbage still clung to her clothes and hair, and exhaustion weighed down her limbs. She'd worked for twenty-two of the past twenty-four hours, was running on gallons of coffee and a twenty minute nap. She wanted a shower, a good meal, and her bed. But karma was a mean bitch and because she'd used the murder call to escape Cam, she now had to go to his house and talk to him about that very same murder.

Dammit.

The stop at her house hadn't exactly been out of her way, nor had it been the most direct route to Cam's, but after leaving the death scene, she hadn't been able to work up enough courage to point her car in his direction.

Okay, so she was procrastinating, but she *did* have to

check on her house's wellbeing. She'd bought the three bed-room, two bathroom, semi-detached Colonial for a ridicu-lously cheap price after the previous owners fell victim to the recession. It had needed major work to make it livable, so what she'd saved in the initial purchase cost, she put to-ward renovations. Now it was exactly as she wanted it—the brick siding clean, no more ugly metal awnings over the win-dows, her little patch of fenced-in yard neatly landscaped with some hardy bushes. Not Home & Gardens worthy, but it was quaint and cozy—a perfect refuge from all the crazi-ness she saw at work.

Except when her sister Shelby or her mother used it as a crash pad between boyfriends.

Shelby had a history of "inviting a few friends over" whenever Eva worked the night shift. But to Shelby, "a few" equaled anything from two to fifty people. For all she knew, her house had been the site of a rave last night. Wouldn't have been the first time.

All appeared quiet from the front, and all of the windows on the closed-in porch were still intact. Promising sign. Maybe Shelby had turned over a new leaf like she claimed.

Okay, Eva really had to get out of the car now. If she stopped moving, she'd crash out for a solid eight hours and she still had to visit Cam.

God, she wished that could wait until morning. With her reserves tapped dry, she'd be more apt to open her mouth and say shit to him she shouldn't. Like, "Hey, that night in Key West? A-ma-zing. What I can remember of it, at least. Wanna try again now that I'm sober?"

Not cool.

Why not? A naughty little voice whispered through her

thoughts. Her damn libido speaking up like the devil on her shoulder. Her angel was conspicuously missing from the other shoulder.

"Because I don't do one night stands," she told it and shoved open the car door. The cold blast of night air did little to perk her up. She climbed out of the vehicle, stretched, but still felt tight all over, her muscles protesting the movement. She needed a good gym session. Or a long night of sex.

It wouldn't be a one night stand anymore if you did it again, the libido devil pointed out.

"I don't do flings, either. Besides, he's my best friend. The alcohol gave me plausible deniability the first time, but if I jumped him again… It's just too weird. Annnd so is arguing with the voice in my head. Oh, Christ, I'm tired. Or crazy. Probably both." She gave herself a full body shake to wake up and hit the car's lock button on the key fob as she trudged through the iron gate in the fence surrounding her yard, up the short walk, and the six concrete steps to her front door.

No music blasting from inside. Also a good sign.

Poe, Shelby's African Grey Parrot, sat in the window and gave a squawk of greeting when she shuffled inside. Smiling, Eva paused to rub his head. She enjoyed Poe and often teased her sister that he was the best boyfriend Shelby's ever had. Poe gently caught her finger in his beak and pulled himself onto her hand, then climbed her arm to her shoulder. She reached up and ruffled the grey feathers on his chest until he chortled and flapped his wings. The sound lifted her spirits, all of her fatigue and worries taking a backseat for the space of a bird's call, and she laughed.

Maybe Poe was her best boyfriend, too.

She crossed the porch, stepped into the living room—and froze. Her sister sat on the couch next to a guy with short, sandy blond hair. A half-eaten box of pizza lay open on the coffee table and *Jeopardy* blared from the TV with the two of them trying to out-geek each other.

"Preston?" Shit. Why hadn't she noticed his car?

He turned and grinned. "Hi. You're home."

"Yeah," she said, drawing the word out. "This is *my* home, right?"

"Of course it is. I just stopped in to see how you're doing."

"I didn't realize our relationship had upgraded to the stop-by-for-the-hell-of-it level. Where's Lark?"

"She had...things..." He waved a dismissive hand. "I was bored and in the neighborhood, so I picked up a pizza and came on by. Is that a crime now, Detective?" he asked with the down-home, Virginia boy smile that used to make her melt. And, okay, it still did a little. Which pissed her off.

Why couldn't she just get over this guy already?

"No," she admitted on an exhale. "But it's getting late and I still have things to do, so you'll have to excuse me for not being Miss Social Butterfly. Shel, can I talk to you for a sec?"

"Sure," Shelby said brightly, but didn't move.

"In. The. Kitchen."

"Oh. Okay." She bounced up from the couch and followed.

As soon they set foot on the black and white tiles of the kitchen floor, Eva whirled on her sister. The fast movement scared Poe, who took flight and landed on top of Shelby's pink-streaked blond ponytail. "Why the fuck did you let him in?"

Frowning, Shelby gathered the bird from her head and set him on his nearby perch. "Hey, he brought pizza and I was hungry. There's no food in the house."

"Oh, dammit, then go shopping! Or— No, that's not even the issue right now." She whirled away, paced a few steps out of utter frustration, then strode to the fridge and jerked it open. "Shelby, I swear, you don't think."

"What?" With her eyebrow ring, tattoos, wild dye-job, and the way she crossed her arms over her chest, she looked more like a rebellious teenager than Eva's younger sister by only ten months. "I thought you were still friends with Preston."

"In the way you and James are still friends."

"Oh." Her brow furrowed. "Wait, which James?"

"Cosplay James."

"Riiight." She winced. "I'm sorry. I didn't know you'd put Preston in the friends-but-not-really category."

"Just…" Finding nothing edible in the fridge, Eva shoved the door shut. "Make him go away. I gotta go back to work."

"Again?"

"For another hour or two. I'll grab some groceries on the way home."

"Okay," Shelby said, heavy on the doubt. "So I should plan to go out for breakfast again?"

"That's not what I said."

"No, but it's what you meant. 'Another hour or two' in Eva Speak means you'll be sleeping at the office again. But," she added before Eva could protest, "I'm okay with eating out. There's this totally hot suit and tie guy that comes into the coffee shop every morning at eight-thirty on the dot.

He's been eying me like he wants to go all ice cream cone on me and lap me up. You know the look, right? The one that says, *yum*? Might be something there."

Eva just barely managed to hold back her groan of frustration. "Don't you think you should give dating a break after the last disaster?"

"Um, no." Shelby's face scrunched with genuine confusion. "Why?"

And that right there was the reason she'd never understand her sister.

"I have to go." With a shake of her head, she decided to exit out the back because dealing with Preston and Cam again in the same night was not something she wanted to do. She made it around the house and was just opening the gate to the driveway when the front door opened and Preston jogged out to meet her.

"Eva, wait."

She didn't even pause as she unlocked her car. "I can't. Work beckons."

"Please. Just…" He vaulted over the gate and slid in between her and the car before she got the door open.

"What?" she snapped.

"I didn't stop by on a whim," he admitted.

No shit. "Then why?"

"I miss you."

"What about Lark?"

"Things…haven't been going well between us since we came home."

"Uh-huh," she said, heavy on the sarcasm.

"Don't be like that. It's not her fault. She's a sweet girl, but she's…not you."

Her heart squeezed. "Preston, don't. Let's not go there."

"I want a second chance."

And he went there. She shoved him. "You *cheated*. You told me you didn't want to get married then turned around and got engaged. How the hell am I ever supposed to trust you again?"

"I know. I'm sorry. I'm an idiot."

"You're not getting an argument from me about that." The tightening around her heart started to hurt, and for a horrifying moment, she feared she'd start crying. She was too tired to deal with this emotional right hook—and she still had to face Cam tonight. "I have to go."

Preston stepped aside and pulled open the car door for her. The perfect gentleman. "Will you think about it?"

No. Yes. God, she had no idea. "I will," she half-lied. "But I can't tonight."

"Fair enough." He waited until she slid in behind the wheel, his arm resting on the top of the door. "Can I call you?"

She shoved the key in the ignition. "I need to go now."

"Right. Okay." He started to lean down, but she saw the kiss coming and shifted the car into gear. He jerked backwards and she took his moment of distraction to grab the door and pull it closed. As she backed out, he stood in the middle of her driveway, his arms crossed over his chest and a frown pulling down the corners of his mouth.

She didn't realize tears streamed down her face until she stopped at the first red light.

Chapter Ten

Eva was the absolute last person Cam expected to find on his porch when he answered the doorbell, and the unexpected punch of seeing her again after days of no voluntary contact from her left him breathless. She looked…exhausted. Her white dress shirt hung wrinkled and untucked from her jeans. Mud coated her boots. She'd given up on any semblance of a fashionable hairstyle and had pulled her straight locks back into a sloppy ponytail that had long since wilted.

She opened her mouth, but no sound emerged.

Cam pulled the door wider. "Want to come in?"

"No." The word sounded forced, as if she had to speak around an obstruction in her windpipe to get it out. She cleared her throat and straightened her shoulders under her favorite leather jacket. "We need to talk."

"Yeah, we do." He scanned the street behind her, half-expecting to see snow because of the bite in the air. Nope, not yet. On its way, though, or so said the talking heads on *The Weather Channel*. The early winter storm was supposed to hit most of the east coast fast and hard, with The District and Baltimore sustaining the brunt of it. The roads would be a mess by morning and although it wasn't yet eight p.m., everything was quiet, everyone tucked up cozy inside their homes in anticipation—the kind of dead stillness that only happened during the wintertime, as if even the city herself was holding her breath waiting for those first flakes to fall.

"I'd prefer to talk inside," Cam said after a drawn out silence. He wore only his sweatpants and an old Air Force T-shirt he'd had since basic training and the cold stung his bare skin. "It's freezing out here."

She hesitated. "Is Vaughn home?"

"No. He's working a case and will probably be at the office most of the night. If not all night. You know how he gets. Dog with a bone."

After another beat of hesitation, she stepped inside. As she passed, the trace scents of recent death and clean snow trailed in behind her. No wonder she was tired. She'd probably been working since he last saw her this morning.

Eva stood in the center of his living room like a stranger who had never been here before. Swung her arms at her sides, then seemed to realize what she was doing and crossed them in front of her.

Yeah, this wasn't awkward at all.

"Have a seat," Cam said and motioned to the only furniture in the room, a giant, L-shaped sectional. When the doorbell rang, he'd been sitting at the end with the built-in recliners, his computer on his lap. He'd spent the day combing through his old cases, trying to figure out who'd want him dead, running checks to see if anyone he'd put away had recently gotten paroled. So far he'd only come up with two names—Arnold Mabry and Tom Lindquist. Mabry was a factory worker who killed his second wife in a fit of passion after finding her in bed with his adult son from his first marriage. He'd made some drunken threats during his arrest, but Cam didn't see him as a real suspect in the murder-for-hire plot. Lindquist, on the other hand, basically beat the system and had all but gotten away with the premeditated murder of his next door neighbor over a property dispute. The guy was a vicious bastard, who still occasionally harassed Cam in subtle ways that stopped just short of being illegal.

Cam would look into them both, but he wasn't convinced of their involvement, and other than those two, he wasn't having much luck with his search. He'd handled a hell of a lot of cases over the years, had pissed off a lot of people, which meant he was in for a lot of digging.

The woman standing in front of him right now was the only person he'd consider asking for help, but he didn't want her involved any more than he wanted his brothers asking around. If the danger was real, it was his to deal with, and he wasn't about to let anybody he cared about get caught in the crossfire.

As casually as possible, he shut the lid on his laptop so Eva wouldn't see the screen.

The TV was on *Investigation Discovery*, but he hadn't been paying much attention to the true-crime show about a serial killer and picked up the remote to shut it off. He regretted it immediately. The sudden lack of background noise only deepened the awkwardness between them and all sorts of off-limit thoughts rushed in to fill the empty silence between his ears. He wanted to scoop her up and take her into his room. Strip her out of those day-old clothes and hold her under the spray of his shower until she relaxed. Help her wash away the remnants of what must have been a hellish day. Then fuck her until she completely forgot about it.

And he was wearing sweatpants. Perfect. No hiding the perky reaction of his cock to those thoughts. He dropped to his seat on the couch. "So what's up?"

Genius, Wilde.

Despite his invitation to sit, Eva stayed rooted where she stood. "I need to get a statement from you."

Cam fumbled the remote still in his hand, caught it before it hit the floor, and set it aside. Okay. Not what he'd expected her to say. "Excuse me?"

"This morning, a 9-1-1 call from a concerned civilian led officers to an empty parking lot, where they discovered a deceased white male slumped beside a Dumpster. We eventually identified him as Steven Donald Goodman, better known as—"

"Soup." Cam's heart plunged into his gut. "Aw, shit. What happened to him?"

Appearing more at ease in her role as detective, Eva finally moved around the end of the couch and sat down—as far from him as she could get and still be on the same piece of furniture. She withdrew a small notepad and pen from an inner jacket pocket. "There was some blood on the scene, but we've concluded it was from a nasty hit to the head when he fell. It appears to be a drug overdose. No other outward signs of trauma besides the head wound, and he presented all the symptoms. But, you know, unattended death. We have to investigate."

"Goddammit." Cam slapped his knee, mostly out of an impotent sense of frustration. But he wasn't surprised. Soup had been on a downward spiral for a while now. It was only a matter of time until this happened.

Except…

At any other time in his acquaintance with Soup, he'd one-hundred percent buy into the death by drug overdose theory. But it was one hell of a coincidence that he'd asked Soup to dig up more information on man who wanted him dead and now Soup was no longer drawing breath.

Too fucking much of a coincidence.

He opened his mouth to tell Eva about it, but clamped his jaw shut without making a sound. If nothing else, Soup's murder told him he was dealing with someone very dangerous, someone who had no qualms about killing whoever stood in the way. He couldn't get her involved in this. Wouldn't take the risk she'd get hurt.

"What I need to know," Eva continued, drawing him back to the conversation, "is why he was wearing your old Carhartt jacket when he died."

Shit. To a suspicious mind, the presence of his jacket on a dead man probably didn't look too good. At least, it wouldn't if he were investigating this case. "How do you know it's mine?"

"Oh, don't even. You wore that thing for how many years?" She rolled her eyes, and he had to hide a smile. This was more like it: Eva falling back into their old habit of friendly bickering, all awkwardness gone.

"I know that jacket when I see it," she added. "The hole in the armpit. Coffee stain on the sleeve. Broken zipper that only you can work. With your connection to him and your habit of giving away your clothes…" She shrugged and crossed her legs, balancing her notebook on her knee. "Doesn't take Sherlock Holmes to figure out where the jacket came from. Since he hadn't sold it for dope yet, I concluded you had contact with him recently. I need an official statement so I can wrap this up, go home, and finally go to bed."

Eva. In bed. Naked.

No, not an appropriate line of thought.

Cam made himself focus on the conversation and not on how good she looked, even wrinkled and muddy, but his gaze kept wandering to her lovely long legs. He remembered the feel of those legs clenched around his hips as he—

"Wilde!" Eva's sharp voice broke through his wandering thoughts. "Focus."

He shook his head to dislodge the fantasy of having her wrapped around him again. But, man, he couldn't seem to help himself.

He wanted her. Still. Always.

Shifting in his seat, he hoped she was far enough away that she wouldn't notice his cock's growing interest. "Uh, yeah." He voice came out rusty and he took a second to clear his throat. "I saw Soup yesterday and gave him the coat."

"All right," she said, her tone much cooler than it had been. And there was the awkwardness again. "What about the five hundred dollars in the pocket?"

His entire attention refocused on the conversation. "How much?"

"Five brand new hundred dollar bills," she said.

Christ. Had Soup accepted a down payment for the hit? A thread of betrayal weaved through his gut even though he shouldn't feel anything at all. Soup hadn't been a friend. Had barely been an acquaintance.

"Do you know where he could have gotten that much?" Eva asked.

"No. I paid him twenty after he gave me some info. As far as I knew, that was all the cash he had."

"What info?" she asked.

Yeah, definitely not telling her that. "Something about the case my brothers and I are working. Nothing major."

"Okay," she said. "So you didn't accidentally leave any money in the jacket?"

"Hell no. I had the two tens in my jeans pocket, that's it. I left my wallet locked in my car, just like I always do when I meet an informant. Besides, I don't often carry around five hundred in cash."

"I didn't think so." She jotted a few notes, then closed her notebook and stood. "Thanks. I need to go write up my report."

She was fast. Almost made it to the door before he caught her wrist. "Whoa. That's it?"

"Yeah." She feigned nonchalance with a shrug. "Like I said, it looks like a straight forward drug overdose. I only needed your statement so I can write up my report. Once we get the toxicology and autopsy results, we can close it out."

"That's not what I meant, Eva."

"I know what you meant," she snapped and twisted out of his grasp. "But I can't deal with…" She waved a hand in the air between them. "This. Us. Not when I've been awake over twenty-four hours and—and with everything else. I can't."

To his complete surprise, tears welled in her eyes, but

they didn't spill over. She'd never let them spill in front of him, and that fucking stung. "Come on, Eva. Talk to me."

"Fine." She met his gaze and her hand settled lightly on his chest. He was ninety-eight percent sure she had no idea it was there, but he sure as fuck knew and his heart damn near leaped out to meet her palm.

"I don't want to lose our friendship," she said matter-of-factly.

Friendship. Right. He exhaled and backed away a step so he could think without her hands on him. Her eyes rounded as if she just realized what she'd been doing, and she crossed her arms over her chest, the tips of her cheeks turning red. He'd always adored that blush. As tough as she was, she could never hide her emotions because her skin showed them all—embarrassment, anger, frustration.

Lust.

Oh, yeah. This particular blush was more lust than anything else. She projected all kinds of I-want-you-naked vibes, and it was driving him crazy because she was so freaked out about it, and he had no idea how to put her at ease.

He cast around for something comforting to say…

And settled on lying through his teeth.

"What are you talking about? We're not gonna lose anything." Even as he laughed it off, he felt like a complete ass. She hated liars, and here he was feeding her the biggest line of bullshit ever. "That night in Key West? It was one night of drunk sex. No big deal."

She dropped her arms to her sides and the splashes of color he loved so much drained right out of her complexion. "I thought…with the things you said…you don't want more than that?"

Fuck yes he did, but not until she was comfortable with the idea. He forced a chuckle, relieved when it came out sounding natural and not like a frog had taken up residence in his throat. "C'mon, you know me. Am I the type of guy to settle down and do the relationship thing? Nah. We're good. Still friends."

Ouch.

No. She shoved away the completely ridiculous spike of pain his words sent spearing through her chest. This was a good thing. He didn't want any kind of relationship with her beyond their friendship. She should be relieved. Dammit, she *was* relieved.

So why the hell was her throat tightening up?

Exhaustion, that's why. She was too damn tired to be having this conversation with him. "I need to go."

As she spun away, his sigh was noisy and full of resignation. "Let me get my jacket."

"What?" She whirled around in time to see him open the closet and pull out a pair of beat-up Nikes, which he slipped his bare feet into, and his new winter coat. Oh, hell no. The whole point of leaving was to escape him. "I'm perfectly capable—"

"It wasn't an offer," he interrupted with a scowl as he stuffed his arms in the sleeves. "It was a statement of fact. You've been awake too many hours to be driving anywhere and I'll feel like shit if you fall asleep at the wheel and kill yourself."

Well, that was a cheery thought. And, she realized, a very

real possibility since her eyelids now weighed about fifty pounds each. "What about my car? I'll need it tomorrow for—"

"I'll drive yours and take a cab home." He picked up his wallet from the foyer table then opened the door for her and stood aside, motioning her to go first.

No sense in trying to talk him out of it. She recognized the mulish expression on his face. His mind was made up and talking him out of anything right now would be like trying to stop the sunrise. Impossible.

Resigned, she walked to the door—and came up short, awed at the blanket of white greeting her. Snow dumped from the sky in huge, heavy flakes, completely covering the street. Already, power lines and tree branches sagged with the weight of it. "Are you fucking kidding me?"

Cam peeked around the edge of the door and clicked his tongue against his teeth. "And the Snow-pocalypse has arrived. We're not going anywhere tonight."

He shut them in together again and a rising sense of panic sent her pacing across the foyer. This cannot be happening. She was only here for twenty, maybe thirty minutes, tops. How could there possibly be that much snow on the ground? "What Snow-pocalypse?"

"Haven't you seen the news?" Sliding out of his coat, Cam strode back to the living room and found the television remote. She followed, dreading what she'd see when he turned on the screen mounted over the fireplace.

Sure enough, the local news featured 24-hour coverage of the winter storm, and from the looks of the radar, it was a big one. Someone needed to smack the Hollywood-handsome meteorologist, who took way too much delight in informing his viewership he expected ten to twelve inches in the next twenty-four hours. Across the bottom of the screen, names of closed buildings and canceled events scrolled by on a red banner. Hell, even a few schools had already decided the mess wouldn't be cleaned up by Monday and had called a snow day.

The city had all but shut down.

This *cannot* be happening!

"But I have to go home. Shelby—she's there by herself. What if the electricity goes out? Worse, what if she decides to throw a no-holds Snow-pocaypse party?"

"Doubt anyone would show if she did." Cam's tone was so reasonable she wanted to throw something at him. How could he be so calm? He slid out of his shoes and returned to his seat on the reclining end of the couch. His laptop sat on the side table next to his bottle of water and a bowl of baby carrots. He popped a carrot in his mouth and grabbed the laptop. "I'm sure she'll be fine."

"Remember last time I left her home alone for a weekend? Five fire departments responded. *Five.*"

"Because the neighbor's house burned down."

"Because Shelby's a walking jinx with no common sense!"

"She'll be fine," Cam said again, still sounding oh-so-reasonable.

"But work—I have to write up the report and—"

"Eva." He finally looked up from his laptop screen. "Give it a rest. You need to shower and sleep, which we both know you were going to do at the station and not at home. Shelby will be fine and the report can wait until the worst of the storm passes. Like you said, Soup's death was a straight-forward drug overdose. Not exactly a high priority rush case. So go shower, borrow some of my sweats to change into. I'll make up your bed." He jerked a thumb toward the high ceiling, where a loft area overhung the living room. The condo had three bedrooms, but he and Vaughn used the third for a weight room, so the office loft had doubled as a guest bedroom whenever she needed to crash at their place.

She hesitated. This was all so…normal. Same as she'd done a hundred times before. Seemed like it shouldn't be this easy to fall back into the patterns of their friendship—not after what happened between them in Key West. But Cam was just so…Cam. Easy-going. Rock-steady. It was hard not to relax around him, and the tightness eased out of her shoulders.

"Fine. Is your comfy Redskins jersey clean?"

"Top drawer." He smiled and there was no heat in his eyes at all, as if that one night had never happened. So he did plan on ignoring the sexual tension between them. He did value their friendship more than the sex.

Thank God.

Okay, she could handle this Cam. This Cam wouldn't slam her against the wall and kiss her until she lost all sense of reason. This Cam wouldn't trap her under his big body and make her feel things that had to be illegal in most states. This Cam wouldn't force her to forfeit her control.

"All right. Thanks," she said and started down the hall. "I'll be out in a few."

In the bedroom, his scent, a mix between his cinnamon gum and the spicy musk unique to him, infused the air. His practical style showed in the no-frills, dark red comforter spread neatly on the king-sized bed. His dresser matched the solid oak of his headboard and he kept his clothes in the wide drawers in no discernible order that she could see, with jeans and T-shirts intermixed with socks and underwear. But, hey, at least he took the time to fold them, which was more than Preston had ever done.

Shit. She didn't want to think about Preston or his plea for a second chance.

Moving fast, she gathered some clothes from the top drawer and scooted into the bathroom, which looked as much like Cam as his bedroom. His scent was stronger in here. A white sink marbled with gray rested on a black cabinet in the center of the room. On the wall over the sink hung a mirror framed in the same black painted wood, and his shaving gear lined the counter underneath it in a tidy row. A nearly full bottle of her favorite brand of hair gel still sat in the exact same spot she'd left it after the last time she'd crashed here. She never thought about it before, but it was sweet of him to buy the gel and the other essentials—disposable razors, deodorant, and even a box of tampons—that he kept under the sink for her.

Before starting the water in the glass-enclosed shower, she used the privacy of the bathroom to call the office, silently hoping they'd need her to come in. No such luck. The duty officer said they were working with a skeleton crew until the storm passed and suggested she "stay home and stay warm."

Well, she'd have no problem staying warm around Cam. She could barely look at him now without heat rushing over her skin and gathering in the center of her belly.

So she tried her sister again, hoping Shelby had managed to find trouble in the short span since she left the house and she'd have to go home and sort it out. And, again, she was S.O.L. Shelby reported that Preston hadn't stuck around, and she and Poe were snuggled in together for a Japanese monster movie marathon.

She ended the call with Shelby, then leaned on the counter and hung her head over the sink in defeat. Tonight was going to be a very, very long night.

Chapter Eleven

Cam popped to his feet as soon as he heard the bath-room door click shut, and did laps around his couch, trying to burn off all the energy vibrating in him. He ached so fiercely to have her again, his muscles trembled from the massive amount of control it had taken to stay seated and appear nonthreatening. Heat licked along every nerve end-ing in his body, leaving him as jittery as an addict jonesing for a hit. He needed a release, preferably one while buried balls-deep inside Eva's hot sex.

And she was in his bathroom right now, stripping off her clothes…

With a string of curses, Cam stopped moving in front of the gas fireplace. He flattened his hands on the mantel and squeezed his eyes shut, his fingers digging into the wood. Had to block out the image of her naked with…some-thing—any-damn-thing else. Baseball. Golf. Yeah, 'cause those two distractions had worked out so well for him in the past. Or the freaking weather. Or maybe the fact that Soup's death sure as hell hadn't been a drug overdose. That should be front and center on his list of concerns, and yet, his mind insisted on torturing him with images of Eva laying on a white bedspread, her hair a cloud of dark silk around her head as he stripped off her red dress… All that bare caramel skin exposed to his mouth and hands…

No, goddammit. He couldn't think about her like that. Obviously their night together had freaked her out, and if he ever wanted a shot at getting her back in his bed, he had to take it slow. Bide his time, give her the opportunity to adjust to the new circumstances of their relationship. He just had to control his body's response around her. Which, going by the massive hard-on he was sporting, was not going to be easy.

Vaughn's bathroom was open. He could run through a quick shower in there with no worries that he'd use any of Eva's hot water because he wanted cold, cold, and colder. Hell, he might even have to go streaking through the storm to douse his need. If he shriveled his boys up far enough, he wouldn't see them again until spring, and he'd be able to face her again like nothing had changed.

And, bright side, they'd only be alone together for a little while. Despite the bad weather, Vaughn would be home at some point—his Hummer laughed in the face of blizzards—and he'd act as a nice damper to the sexual tension. A kind of built-in cockblock.

So, shower. Then maybe Vaughn would be home and he wouldn't be able to act on his fantasies.

Cam took two steps toward Vaughn's bedroom, and his cell phone rang. He backtracked and picked it up off the end table, where it had been charging. Vaughn's name showed on the caller ID, and Cam shook his head. He probably should have expected it—he'd been thinking about his twin, after all. Sometimes even he got spooked by how in tune they were.

He answered. "Hey, bro. Have you looked outside recently?"

"Yeah, it's nasty," Vaughn said, "and getting worse. The Hummer can probably handle it, but the city's got a ban on unnecessary travel, so I'm crashing at Greer's until the ban's lifted."

Damn. There went his cockblock. Greer lived in an apartment complex several blocks over from the Wilde Security office and, yeah, it was probably better that Vaughn stayed there for the night.

Still…

Damn.

"You okay?" Vaughn asked.

He heaved a sighed. "Eva's here."

Vaughn's laughter boomed over the line. "Well, you have the house to yourselves for the night. Feel free to dirty up every available surface—uh, except my bed. And if you fuck on the kitchen counter, don't tell me about it."

"You're not helping."

"Really? I thought that was very helpful advice."

"Vaughn," he said in exasperation. "She only stopped to ask me questions about one of my former informants and now she's stuck here because of the storm. She won't say it, but she's bugged out by what happened in Key West."

"So take her to bed. If you keep her busy, she won't have time to bug out about anything. Seems simple enough to me."

"Only because you tend to think with the head in your pants, not the one on your shoulders."

"Mm. Your point?"

Cam grumbled. "Someday, you're gonna meet a woman who gets you so twisted around you won't know which way is up. Then I'll sit back and laugh."

"Yeah, right."

"Famous last words, bro. Didn't I hear a rumor you caught the garter at Jude's wedding? Who was the lucky lady to catch the bouquet?"

A pause. "Lark."

"Ah ha. And afterward, you hit on her and she wasn't interested because she's already engaged to that asshole Linz. No wonder you were in such a shitty mood that night. You're not used to women telling you to get lost."

Vaughn growled low in his throat. "Something like that."

"Oh yeah, that's the first sign. Hate to tell ya, but your days of fast women are numbered."

"Shut the fuck up and go deal with your own woman."

The line went dead and Cam found himself grinning as he set down the phone. If he didn't know any better, Vaughn was already twisted up about someone.

Lark?

Hmm. Something to consider later.

At least the phone call had calmed him down in the way that a cold shower wouldn't have. He could handle this situation with Eva. And maybe Vaughn did have a point. He had spent five long years in the role of best friend. It was time to step up his game and make it absolutely clear friendship wasn't enough for him anymore. He wouldn't push too hard, but if he backed off completely, he'd never get anywhere with her.

He heard the water stop running through the pipes and strode into the kitchen. He'd planned to just snack his way through dinner tonight, but Eva needed something more than a bowl of carrots. Opening the fridge, he considered the contents against his mental list of meals he could make without giving her food poisoning. Hmm. Probably best to stick to canned food. Reece was the only half-way decent cook in the family. He moved on to the cupboards and found a family-sized can of SpaghettiOs. That would work.

By the time he heard Eva's bare feet coming down the hallway, he had the can open and was in the process of dumping it into a pot on the stove. She wore his Redskins jersey and a pair of sweats that had shrunk in the dryer, but he kept around for her.

With her hair down around her shoulders and sleek with water from her shower, she looked vulnerable. Not like a child, because the jersey clung to her obviously bare breasts and her nipples stood out invitingly under the nylon mesh. More like a woman unsure of herself.

Was she self-conscious because of him?

As much as he craved her, he didn't want her feeling insecure around him. This wasn't his Eva, the woman who unapologetically kicked ass—his included—and didn't take shit from anybody. The woman who could out-drink almost any man he knew. Who trounced him at darts on a regular basis and threw down at the gym like her life depended on flooring him. Who called him on his bullshit, but got his sense of humor and laughed at his jokes when nobody else did. Where was that woman? Because she wasn't standing in his kitchen right now, and pain sliced through him with the knowledge he was responsible for sending her into hiding.

He wanted his Eva back.

"Hey there." He returned his attention to his task, scraping out the last bit from the can with a spoon. "Making my world famous SpaghettiOs for dinner."

"World famous?" With a derisive snort, she sat at the island bar that separated the kitchen from the living room. "Someone's stroking his own ego."

Not exactly the kind of stroking he wanted, but if it got her to smile, he'd take it. At least now she was comfortable enough to joke with him. That was a good sign. "Aw, ouch. I thought you like my canned goods. There's even meatballs."

"Pleading the fifth."

He gave the pot a stir. "Well, as Dad used to say, you'll eat it and like it or go without—and you're not going without."

Eva smiled and visibly relaxed, her shoulders easing up underneath the jersey. "Have I ever mentioned how much I think I would have liked your dad?"

"He would have loved you, no doubt in my mind about it. He always wanted a daughter, but after Jude turned out to be another boy, my parents called it quits with the baby making."

"Good thing. The world can't handle more Wilde boys."

He took a couple bowls down from the cupboard. "If Dad had a daughter, he would have treated her like just another one of the boys. She would have turned out a lot like you—except with better rhythm. Mom being a dance instructor and all."

"A monkey has better rhythm than I do, so that's not saying much."

The SpaghettiOs done, Cam dumped some into one of

the bowls and set it in front of her, then stepped over to the Keurig and opened the lid. "Coffee?"

She stared at it with obvious longing, but then shook her head. "Better not. I don't think anything will keep me awake at this point, but I'd rather not take the chance."

"Right." He popped a K-cup into the machine for himself, grabbed his favorite mug from the dish drainer, and discovered he was fresh out of small talk. There were so many things he wanted to say to her—"I love you" chief among them—but that wouldn't put her at ease around him so he kept his mouth shut. After all these years, he was damn good at keeping mum.

Cam busied himself with dishing up his own bowl. More than once, he swore he felt her eyes on him like a stroking hand down his ass, but whenever he turned around, she'd be staring down at her food. When his bowl was filled, he picked up his coffee and joined her at the bar.

Silence spread between them, thick and more impenetrable by the minute.

Finally, Eva pushed her half-eaten dinner away. "I'm going to bed."

The way she said it, he couldn't decide if it was an invitation or a warning. He nodded. "I haven't made up the pull-out yet."

"I know where everything is." She stood. "Mind if I skip helping with dishes tonight?"

"No problem. I got them."

"Thanks for cooking for me," she said but still didn't move.

Cam set down his fork. "Eva. Are we going to be okay?"

Sleepy eyes traced over his face, down his body, and

lingered on his lap. There was no hiding his response to the once over with the pop tent action going on at the front of his pants. Dammit, couldn't he have a civil conversation with this woman without his cock leaping to attention?

She hissed out a breath and spun away.

"Eva," he called.

She paused with one hand on the ladder to the loft and met his gaze from across the room. "I don't know, Cam. I really…don't know."

Chapter Twelve

Eva found cotton sheets for the pull-out bed in an old trunk that Cam had once told her belonged to his mother. She fitted them on the mattress before settling down and shutting her eyes. With how tired she was, she expected to fall right into dreamland, but she was far too aware of Cam's every movement in the rooms below. He wasn't loud. In fact, he seemed to be going out of his way to stay quiet, and she only heard a few clinks of silverware against the sink basin as he cleaned up.

Was it too much to hope that he'd retire to his room when he finished? Probably. It was still too early for a night owl like him to go to bed and, sure enough, he settled down on the couch in the living room a few minutes later. The TV clicked on, and he immediately lowered the sound to little more than a muffled whisper, then he shut off the lights.

Eva lay on her back for a long time, watching the blue flicker of the TV against the far living room wall. Sleep completely eluded her and, instead, her mind wandered to places it shouldn't go.

Like to Cam, naked, his erection straining toward her…

Damn. She kicked off the blanket and sheet. Every muscle in her body ached as if she'd spiked a fever, stress coiling tighter and tighter inside her with each passing minute. She yearned for a release, but a repeat of Key West wasn't going to happen. Couldn't happen. Cam was so far off limits, he might as well be on a different planet. He'd made it plenty clear the sex had just been sex, and although his body may still respond to her, she wasn't anyone he wanted long-term. He didn't want anything more than their friendship.

Didn't mean she didn't still want more of *him*.

The man himself was off limits, yes. But how many times had she fantasized about him over the years? Little forbidden treasures she kept tucked away and brought out only on the longest, loneliest nights. She could pop the lid off the pressure cooker of sexual tension inside her, and nobody had to know who was front and center in her imagination when she did.

Heart pounding, she slid her hand over her belly and bit down on her lower lip as her fingers dipped under the waistband of her panties.

Cam's head snapped up at the soft groan and he muted the TV, his eyes scanning the loft overhead. Was Eva having a bad dream? Should he go up and wake her? He hated to when she so badly needed the sleep, but if she was having nightmares, she'd wake up more exhausted than before she went to bed.

She moaned softly again and heat licked down his spine. That sound was all sexy, aroused woman—definitely not from a nightmare—and his cock filled in anticipation.

Was she getting herself off?

Closing his eyes, he pictured her on the bed upstairs, knees lifted and parted under the sheet as her fingers dipped in and out of her tight pussy.

He shuddered and wrapped one hand around his shaft, squeezing hard to keep back the release tightening his balls. He told himself to chill out, let her do what she needed to do to help her relax. Intruding on this private moment of hers would only make things more awkward between them come morning.

"Cam…"

His name, barely a breath of air on her lips, echoed in the silence of the house. He wasn't entirely sure she even knew it had escaped, but fuck, he liked it. Would never get tired of hearing her call it while lost in the grip of sexual satisfaction. Wanted to hear it again and again, preferably as he drilled so deep she forgot everything but his name.

Fuck it.

He lay back against the couch cushion. Splayed his legs and tucked the front of his pants under his balls, giving himself better access as he strained to hear every sweet sound Eva made. He pumped his hand up and down his cock, slow at first, then harder, faster, until he shook with the need to come.

And the next time he heard her soft moan of pleasure, he was right there with her.

B usted.
　　Eva froze at the erotic growl from downstairs and then flushed even hotter. She should be embarrassed at getting caught masturbating. She wasn't. Instead, the heat came from straight-up, no holds lust.

Cam had his hand on himself, too.

She wished she could see him working himself, that big hand wrapped tight around his thick cock, his back arching into each downward movement, his hard stomach muscles contracting, the cords in his neck taut as he strained toward release.

Oh, God.

The mental image pushed her closer to her own orgasm and she gasped, every sensation amplified tenfold. Her breasts felt full and heavy, her nipples scraping almost painfully against the nylon mesh of Cam's jersey. Her thighs trembled hard enough to make the pull-out bed shake. So, so close. She just needed…something…more…

"Eva." Cam's voice was a rasp against her nerve endings in the silence. "Come for me. I want to hear you."

The rubber band tension snapped and she orgasmed hard, gasping and shuddering through it. Cam's rough shout of release echoed off the ceiling and joined the involuntary sounds of pleasure spilling from her own lips.

And then, silence again.

Spent, Eva let her legs fall straight even as tiny aftershocks wracked her body. She'd never before felt anything so intense by herself. Then again, she wasn't alone this time.

Not really. She turned her head on the pillow to look through the loft's railing at the empty space over the living room. The TV still flickered against the wall in muted shades of blue. She couldn't see Cam from where she lay, but imagined him sprawled on the couch, his skin slick with sweat, chest heaving to draw in air. She bet he made a beautiful sight, all sexy, sated male. Too bad she didn't have the energy to stand up and actually get a look at him.

As her eyes drifted shut, she swore she heard him murmur, "Goodnight, sweetheart."

Warmth suffused her chest and, smiling, she tumbled into sleep.

Chapter Thirteen

That was a *helluva* lot more than ten inches of snow.

Cursing under her breath, Eva closed the door on the knee-high drift making Cam's front porch impassible without a shovel, and leaned her forehead against the cool wood. She knew her car sat in his driveway, but she'd be hard pressed to find it at the moment. Even if she could get to it and somehow dig it out with her hands—her *bare* hands because she hadn't thought to bring gloves with her last night—there was still nowhere to drive. Covered in an even white blanket, the street looked no different from the sidewalk or his neighbors' yards.

So much for making a stealthy escape before Cam woke up.

And after last night, the thought of facing him made her stomach jitter.

Christ, she didn't know what was wrong with her. Why, all of the sudden, she couldn't keep her hands off him—or, apparently, herself—whenever she thought about him. It had never been like this with Preston or the few other men she'd dated. She always knew where she stood with them, because she'd always called the shots in their relationship, both in bed and out. But Cam left her off-balance, reeling until she had no idea who stood where. It freaked her the hell out.

So she had to gain control. She had to stop avoiding him and let him know in no uncertain terms that friendship is all she wanted from him, too, despite what happened in Key West. And last night.

Actually, she wouldn't mention last night at all. Too embarrassing.

She kicked off her shoes and hung her jacket on the rack by the door, then padded back to the living room and checked the digital clock on the cable box. The storm hadn't taken out their electricity, and the clock changed from 7:59 to 8:00 AM as she watched. Cam wouldn't be up for another hour at least. Maybe two. He'd never been much of a morning person. She scanned the condo's open floor plan, not entirely sure what to do with herself, and spotted her bag where she'd left it propped against the side of the couch.

Work. That's what she'd do.

Feeling steadier now that she had a purpose, she scooped up the bag and settled at the kitchen breakfast bar. She had copies of some files she needed to review before the cases went to court, so she brought the folders out, spreading them on the counter. She picked one at random, opened the cover, and was greeted by gruesome crime scene photos.

The tension bunching her muscles eased away as she threw herself into the work. What did it say about her that murder was so much easier to handle than the feelings Cam stirred up? She shuddered to think. So she stopped thinking altogether—at least about him—and focused on the intricacies of the difficult investigation laid out step-by-step in the report before her.

S he didn't notice him right away, which was fine by Cam. He didn't get to see her with her guard down much anymore, and he stopped short in the hallway outside his bedroom to watch her. She hunched over a file on the counter, her lips moving a little as she read the contents. Then she sat up, brow furrowed, and flipped the pages.

He loved watching her work. Back when they'd been partners, how many times had he caught himself staring at her? In fact, how many times had *she* caught him staring? He always made a dumb excuse or cracked a joke so she wouldn't know exactly the kinds of thoughts in his head as he watched her. Well, no more.

He purposely bumped his elbow into the wall and her head snapped up.

"Oh." She shuffled her files together, her back and shoulders tightening up again with each step he took toward her. "How long have you been standing there?"

"A few minutes."

"Why didn't you—"

"Because I wanted to watch you."

She snorted. "That's not creepy."

All right, so she'd resorted to cracking the jokes this time. He ignored it. "Did you sleep?"

The color filling her cheeks about matched the red of the coffee mug he pulled out of the cupboard.

"Yes," she said stiffly.

"Did you eat yet?" He opened the freezer, found a box of Eggo waffles, and filled the four-slotted toaster.

"Uh, no." She shifted around uncomfortably, no doubt trying to think of an escape plan as he left the waffles to cook and fixed himself a cup of coffee. He never felt fully functional until he got that kick of caffeine and sighed in pleasure with the first sip.

"What are you doing?" Eva demanded when he opened his eyes again.

"Cooking breakfast."

She crossed her arms in front of her. "You don't have to cook for me."

"Uh, I usually do when you stay over. Outta the two of us, I'm better with a toaster. Which, granted, isn't saying much for either of us, but you never had a problem with it before."

Her mouth opened, then snapped shut. "I'm not hungry."

"Bullshit." He set his mug on the counter, smacking it against the granite harder than he'd planned. But, c'mon, she was being so freaking obstinate this morning, and frustration rumbled through him. "You're *always* hungry."

As if to prove his point, her stomach growled loud enough for him to hear it. Arching his brow, he returned to the coffee maker to start her cup. She let him finish making their breakfast without further comment, nursing her coffee in a broody silence.

Ten minutes later, he slid a plate of waffles and micro-waved bacon to her and she dug in like she was aiming for first place in an eating competition, obviously in a hurry to get away from him. So, naturally, he sat on the stool beside her. She shifted away, giving him her shoulder.

What were they, middle schoolers? C'mon.

Exasperated, he stabbed at a piece of waffle and the tongs of his fork clanged against the plate each time he went back for another bite. He wanted to say something, but anything that came out of his mouth would either piss her off or send her fleeing in terror, so he kept his jaw clamped. Which made eating difficult. Each new bite was more and more like gnawing on cement.

About half-way through the silent meal, she slowed, picking at her food instead of devouring it. Then she stopped.

"Dammit, I hate this awkwardness," she blurted and threw her fork at her plate. She turned to him, a plea in her dark eyes. "Cam, I don't want to lose our friendship over one night."

"I already told you it was just sex," he muttered. "Not a big deal."

"But nothing has been the same between us. I miss you."

He exhaled and set down his own fork. "I miss you, too."

"Good. Then let's put this behind us and — "

"No."

She sat back like he'd hauled off and punched her. "What?"

Fuck it. He was done biding his time. He'd thought it was the right move with how nervous she was, but last night proved she wanted him just as much as he wanted her.

"Things can't go back to the way they were between us." He let all the desire he had for her show on his face. His voice roughened, and if she glanced down at his lap, she'd get an eyeful. He was so hard, the tip of his cock peeked out the top of pants, and he didn't bother hiding it. "Every time I see you, I remember how fucking amazing the sex was and I want more of it. I didn't get enough that night."

Eva dropped her head into her arms on the counter and groaned. "See, this is why I've been avoiding you. I didn't want to have this conversation. Not with you."

"Can you tell me you haven't replayed Key West in your mind over and over again until you're so wound up you have to do something about it? Isn't that what happened last night?"

Color infused her cheeks again when she looked up, and that was all the answer he needed. Yes, she'd gotten herself off on her memories more than once since returning home.

She ducked her head, her hair falling forward to shield her face. "Last night was…"

"What? A mistake? A fluke? A bad idea? Yeah, probably, but you can't blame alcohol this time because we were both stone cold sober. I knew exactly what I was doing. I wanted it. Hell, I wanted to climb the ladder and see you touching yourself, taste you as you came, then fuck you until neither of us could walk." Her flinch made him feel like a jerk, but he'd had enough of second guessing himself and censoring his words. This tap dance they'd been doing around each other since returning home had gotten old. If she was stuck here for a few days, they were going to hash this out right now. "Tell me you didn't want that, too."

She straightened in her seat and met his gaze, her eyes full of her damned stubborn pride. "I didn't. I don't. Not with you."

"You've never had much of a poker face, Cardoso."

"Cam…" she said his name faintly, almost an imploration. He shook his head, cutting off any excuses she might try to make. He wasn't in the mood for them.

"I'm sorry. That's where we stand, and we can't go back."

Walking out of the kitchen was the hardest thing he had ever done, knowing that this might be the end of their friendship and he'd never see her again when the snowstorm ended. But she had to make a choice and she couldn't do it with him hanging around, riling her up.

He shut himself in the en suite off his bedroom and leaned on the sink, refusing to let the sense of defeat rising in his chest get him down. She wanted him as much as he did her. He knew it without a shred of doubt. So why was it so damn hard for her to admit?

"She'll come around," he told his reflection. He just had to be patient a little longer.

But, fucking hell, after five years he was nearly out of patience.

Groaning at himself, he shoved away from the sink and stripped off his sweatpants. He started the shower and jumped in without checking the water temp, welcoming the blast of ice over his head until his nipples pebbled, goose bumps prickled across his skin, and his boys threatened shrinkage. Only then did he adjust the water to a more comfortable temperature, but that was as far as he got. A hot shower wasn't the kind of heat he'd wanted when he woke up this morning. Stupid of him to hope for more from her, but after last night's mutual masturbation session, he had.

She'd called his name as she came. And he imagined her doing it again as he pounded mercilessly into her, punishing her for making him so crazy.

His cock strained out from his body, looking for something it wasn't going to get any time soon. He wrapped a hand around his shaft, stroking it none too gently, punishing himself for wanting something he shouldn't. But, yeah, his heart wasn't in it. Besides, there was something sleazy about whacking off in the shower when the object of his desire sat in the other room. Disgusted, he reached for the bar of soup—

And the bathroom door opened.

Holy shit. He almost didn't dare look and turned slowly, afraid he might spook her. Through the steaming glass of the shower door, he watched her strip off her shirt and drop it beside his pants. Next, she reached around to unclasp her bra and that hit the floor, too, her nipples pebbling in the humid air. He swallowed a groan as she slid her thumbs into the waistband of her sweatpants and pushed them down. She wasn't wearing panties.

She pulled open the shower door, but hesitated and lifted her gaze to his.

This was it, the part where she'd start worrying and second guessing. He saw the indecision in her eyes and braced himself for the sting of yet another rejection. If she ran this time, he would not chase her. If she ran... Well, that would probably be the death of everything good between them.

"I want you, too," she said and stepped into the shower, closing the door firmly behind her.

Chapter Fourteen

"Stop," Cam said, and her stomach dropped like on the first hill of a roller coaster. Had she waited too long? Had he rethought his ultimatum during the five minutes she'd paced the living room, warring between desire and her common sense?

Heat that had nothing to do with the water pouring from the showerhead reddened her face and neck. Dammit, she wished she was better at controlling that fucking blush. It always gave away feelings she'd rather keep to herself.

"Do you want me to go?" She was already reaching for the door, but his hand shot out and caught her wrist.

"Eva, don't."

She stared up at him, confused by the touch of desperation in his words.

"If you run…" He couldn't seem to finish the sentence, but he didn't have to. She saw it in his eyes. If she left now, they were done. Completely done. No more superhero movie marathons or Sunday football games or karaoke nights. No more drinking games or crazy bets. No more Cam.

Her chest constricted. "I don't want to run, but you told me to leave."

"I told you to stop," he said, voice rough. He let go of her wrist and dropped to his knees in front of her. The water beat down on his head, streamed over his face, but he didn't seem to care. "As in, stop moving. You can't touch me yet. I'm too wound up and I want to see you." His breath fanned her stomach moments before his lips teased the skin there and his tongue flicked out to play around her bellybutton. He slid lower, nipping her hip with his teeth as one hand parted her legs, strong male fingers brushing lightly back and forth over her entrance. She gasped and arched toward him, clutching the towel bar on the wall behind her for support.

Cam kissed his way up her bowed body until his mouth found hers. "You're already wet for me," he whispered against her lips. His fingers parted her and drew circles around her clit. She trembled and his other hand circled her waist, steadying her.

"Do you want to come now?" He gave the sensitive nub a tweak that sent lightning bolts of pleasure zig-zagging across her vision.

"Yes, yes, yes." The sounds coming from her throat were like nothing she'd ever heard from herself before, and she didn't give a damn. She rocked into his hand, wanting more of those talented fingers, but he drew away, chuckling into her mouth before sealing his lips to hers in a flaming hot kiss.

"Or maybe I'll draw it out," he said and tugged on her lower lip with his teeth. "Make you wait. Beg for it."

"Don't you dare," she gasped. "I'll hurt you."

He laughed. "How? I seemed to have you pinned."

And he did, her back plastered to the tile wall with one of his hands holding both of her wrists captive over her head, her thighs parted by his hips. How did that happen? But she didn't get a chance to freak out over how fast she'd lost control of the situation, because his mouth found hers again, his fingers hit all the right spots between her thighs, and pleasure blinded her to everything else but the man in front of her.

His lips traced a hot path along her jaw to her ear. "You're gonna wait," he told her even as he caressed her clit again. Overloaded with sensation, her leg muscles gave out. She would have collapsed if not for him holding her up.

"Yeah, you're gonna wait. Know why?"

She shook her head, her wet hair sticking to her cheeks. Jaw set, Cam let go of her wrists and turned her so that she faced the wall. His hand traced the curve of her spine, cupped her ass, then left her. She glanced over her shoulder, watching him take himself in hand and guide the flared head to her opening.

His breath hissed out between clenched teeth, and his chest heaved as he pushed inside. "You're gonna wait be-cause I want to feel your pussy squeezing me when you come."

He pumped his hips, slow at first and then faster, harder until she lost all sense of herself. All that mattered was their connection and the growing sense of pressure building in her core. She pushed back, meeting his thrusts with her own, needing him even deeper.

When he reached around and found her clit again, she shattered, screaming his name. Behind her, Cam roared with satisfaction, his body spasming with his own release.

Then, silence. Except for their sawing breaths and the water splattering against the tile floor.

Cam leaned over and pressed a kiss to the base of her neck before dislodging their bodies. She shivered, half from the chill of having been out of the warm water for too long, and half from the sensation of loss as he pulled out. He gathered her into his arms, her back secure against his hard chest, and switched their positions so that the water rained down on her. She shut her eyes, relaxed into him, and allowed him to run the soap over her sensitive breasts and belly. For a short moment, she felt more secure than she ever had in her life. Cared for. Loved, even.

Her eyes snapped open. Hell to the no. That's not what this was about. She wasn't looking for love anymore. Growing up, she'd yearned for a perfect life. She'd watched TV and imagined herself in those happy families. Later, in college, she made one up so she never had to tell anyone the truth of her upbringing. But when she thought of her four oldest siblings growing up in loving homes with doting parents, jealousy ate her up inside. She'd wanted that. Still wanted it in her weaker moments.

It was just a pipe dream, though. She wasn't built for that kind of love, and the one glimmer of hope she'd had died in Key West when she found out Preston had cheated on her. So this thing between her and Cam was not about love. Just friendship and sex, plain and simple.

But did Cam know that? The way he was handling her, like something extremely precious to him, suggested not.

She shrugged out of his arms and faced him, the water beating on her back beginning to run cool. "We need to set some boundaries."

His brows slammed together. "Uh, don't ya think we just smashed through all the boundaries?"

"Exactly why we need new ones."

Cam's jaw tightened, then he reached around her to shut the water off and opened the shower door. "I have a feeling we should get dressed for this conversation."

She nodded and followed him from the shower. Wordlessly accepted the towel he offered and tucked it around herself as he went to the linen closet to get another one. His back to her, he dragged his towel through his hair, did a quick run with it down his front and backside, then wound it around his hips and faced her again. The green terrycloth dipped in front to show off the V of muscle at his hips and highlighted his still semi-hard erection. Her eyes traced the length of him—couldn't help herself. Who would have guessed under his laid-back, jeans and T-shirt style, Cam was an all-around physically impressive male specimen?

She moistened her lips, and lust flared hot in his eyes before he strode toward the door.

"I think I have a pair of your jeans from the last time you crashed here," he said over his shoulder. "I can give you a T-shirt to wear while your clothes from yesterday wash."

She bent to retrieve the Redskins jersey she'd worn as a nightshirt and pulled it on over her towel. "It's fine. I'll wear this."

He glanced back, did a double take as the towel pooled around her feet, and made a low rumbling sound deep in his throat. He turned to his dresser, tore through it with a renewed sense of urgency, and tossed a pair of pants at her. She caught them. Her favorite slouchy jeans.

"So that's where these went. I've been looking for them."

"You spilled coffee on yourself last time you were over and I threw them in the washer. You left without them."

"Oh yeah. Forgot about that." She stepped into the soft denim and buttoned the waistband, then remembered she wasn't wearing a bra and backtracked to the bathroom to put it on. By the time she returned to the bedroom, the door stood open and Cam's towel lay abandoned at the foot of his bed. She found him in the kitchen, wearing another pair of his endless supply of sweatpants and no shirt.

As he busied himself with making yet another cup of coffee, she took the opportunity to study his hard-cut muscles, highlighted by the tribal swirls of his shoulder tattoo. Funny, she'd seen him shirtless plenty of times in the past, and never once had the thought "gorgeous sex god" popped into her head. Now, it wouldn't leave. She considered walking up behind him and tracing the indent of his spine with her tongue…

No. Talk first.

Then, if it went well, they'd see about more sex.

"All right, what kind of boundaries?" Cam dumped his cold coffee from breakfast in the sink, then settled against the counter with the fresh mug in hand. His front view was even sexier than the back, flat copper nipples pebbled in the cool air, abs and pecs more often seen on fitness models than ex-homicide detectives, and an intriguing trail of hair pointing from his shallow bellybutton to the waistband of his pants, which tented when her gaze zeroed in on the bulge there.

He shifted and cleared his throat.

Shit, she had to stop doing that.

Eva returned to her seat at the island bar, pushing away the breakfast plate she'd left when she chased him into the shower. "Well, obviously things have changed between us since Key West."

"Obviously," he said, deadpan, and lifted his mug to his mouth. "You never used to eye-fuck me like you just were."

Heat crept up the back of her neck. "Right. And we're both single and unattached…"

"Uh-huh. So what are you saying?"

"The sex is…" God, she couldn't think of a word. Amazing wasn't high enough praise but, really, did she want to stroke his ego like that? If she did, she'd never hear the end of it, so she started over. "I wouldn't mind continuing our physical relationship."

One dark brow arched, and his lips twisted into a wry smile. "You wouldn't mind?"

"Oh, hell. I *want* to continue, but we can't let sex ruin our friendship. We're friends first, and if this chemistry between us is going to change that, then I'm not willing to give up our friendship for a few good nights together."

"I'd like a lot more than a few."

Oh boy, so would she. Especially when he stood there with his hair still damp, looking…lickable, as Shelby would say. Yeah, it was the only term to describe him right now. Mouthwatering and gorgeous and completely lickable.

Pretending nonchalance, she shrugged. "We'll have to wait and see how it goes, but if it ever starts to interfere with us, it ends. Deal?"

He considered it for so long, her stomach began to flutter with nerves. But, finally, he finished his coffee, pushed away from the counter, and stood across the island from her. "Before I agree, there's something else we need to talk about."

For the life of her, she couldn't begin to guess what that something was, but the seriousness of his expression chilled her. "Okay."

"I don't know how to ask this tactfully, so I'll just come out and... Aw, damn." He rubbed his jaw, his beard stubble rasping against his palm, then met her gaze. "Could you be pregnant?"

She sat back, her head reeling as if he'd just dealt her a physical blow. "What?"

"I ask because if so, that changes everything. We didn't use a condom in there." He tilted his head, indicating the direction of his bedroom. "Honestly, it's been so long for me, I don't even know if I have any condoms in the house. And I don't exactly remember, but pretty sure we skipped the safe sex discussion in Key West, too."

She blew out a breath, taking the moment to calm her racing heart. "No, I'm not pregnant. I'm on birth control."

"Even though you've been single?"

"Let me clarify, I'm *always* on birth control, single or not. I don't make a habit of one-night-stands, but shit happens — like Key West, for example — and I refuse to end up like my mother with nine kids by eight different fathers."

Cam's eyes widened. "I didn't know you had any siblings besides Shelby."

"They were placed in foster care before Shelby or I came along. We're ten months apart and have different fathers, but by the time we were born, CPS was sick of finding homes for Mom's kids and decided she had *settled down* enough to raise us."

Eva winced at the bitterness so very evident in her words. Some of her siblings had gone to good homes and were doing all right for themselves now. Others had ended up in worse situations than she'd grown up in and were either dead or in prison. She supposed she should count herself lucky she didn't end up with foster parents who could care less about her—because for all of her mother's faults, nobody could ever say Katrina didn't love her children when she was sober.

"I stay on birth control," she said, evening her voice out, "because any kids I have will be wanted, planned for. They'll have embarrassing baby photos and college funds. Their lives are going to be as close to that perfect 1950s sitcom family as possible."

She couldn't stand to see the sorrow in Cam's expression and dropped her gaze to the counter. Up until his parents died, he'd had the life she'd always wanted, and a secret part of her, tucked away deep inside the darkest chambers of her heart, had always hated him for it. "So, um, we're safe. No surprise babies."

Cam watched her across the island, and she had to fight to keep from fidgeting under his scrutiny. After a minute that seemed like an hour, he nodded. "Good. Takes a weight off."

Okay, she definitely shouldn't experience a pang of hurt that he was relieved about there being almost no possibility of pregnancy. Yet, there it was, digging claws into her heart.

Fucking hell. Was there a prize for most emotionally wrecked? If not, there should be. She'd win it, hands down.

Chapter Fifteen

He'd always known Eva's childhood hadn't been a cake walk, but she'd never before offered up any details, and he'd never asked. Now, Cam knew without doubt the small glimpse she'd just given wasn't the worst of it, and his heart broke for the little girl she'd once been.

He finished his coffee in a hard swallow and hoped like hell she didn't notice the tremble of his hand as he set the mug in the sink. Fucking child services should have done more to protect her and Shelby, and the fact they had failed the two girls so miserably pissed him off in a big way.

He needed to pummel something. Like, right fucking now. "I'm gonna hit the gym."

Eva shook herself from whatever internal demons she'd been battling, and her gaze refocused on the here and now. She frowned. "But you just showered."

"So, I'll shower again." He couldn't stand around chatting with her, not with the ball of useless anger at her mother and the flawed child care system eating at his gut.

Without waiting for her response, he left the kitchen and strode past the doors of his and Vaughn's rooms to the master bedroom at the end of the hall, which they'd elected to convert to a gym when they moved in because of its massive size. His feet sank into the padded mats covering the floor as he crossed to a line of shelves along one wall and grabbed his fingerless boxing gloves from their spot on the third shelf. Flexing his hands to make sure they fit correctly, he finally let the anger explode in a burst of movement. He spun and nailed the nearby heavy bag with a roundhouse that sent it swinging.

Child *protective* services. Protection was their job, goddammit.

And fuck Eva's mother for living the kind of selfish lifestyle that made their half-hearted intervention necessary in the first place.

Cam lit into the bag, attacking it from every angle until his knuckles ached and sweat blinded him, but the anger still sat like molten lead in the pit of his soul. His mind kept conjuring up the image of a small, dark haired girl watching *Full House* with longing in her big, dark eyes as her mother lay passed out on the couch from another round of binge partying, and it just added more fuel to the fire of his rage. He didn't stop until he hit the bag so hard, it swung back and plowed into his stomach. Air left his lungs in a whoosh, and with it, finally, his anger. He bent double, placing his hands on his knees and dragging in lung-filling drafts of air.

"Feel better?"

He straightened, not all that surprised to see Eva propped in the doorway. "No."

She crossed her arms over her chest. "Listen, I'm sorry if I pissed you off, but if you want to continue sleeping together, those are my terms."

"What?" He stared at her, his mind backtracking over their conversation before her past came up. "Shit. No, that's not — I'm good with that." Well, mostly. Friends with benefits wasn't exactly what he'd wanted, but it was a step in the right direction. "I mean, no strings sex between friends? What's not to like?"

Eva nodded toward the punching bag. "So why go all Hulk on that thing?"

Because she'd deserved better than what she'd gotten, and there wasn't a damn thing he could do to change the past.

He shrugged. "Needed a workout."

"The athletic shower sex wasn't workout enough for you?"

Yeah, it had been, and he'd pay for all the abuse he'd subjected his muscles to this morning. "Nah. I'm foggy if I don't get in a good session with the bag." He unstrapped his gloves and discovered not only had he beat his knuckles raw, but his fingers had stiffened up. Fuck, that was going to hurt in a few hours. He returned the gloves to their spot and casually shook out each hand before bending to grab a water from the mini fridge on the bottom shelf. "So…have you checked the weather reports?"

Great. Now he'd stooped to small talk about the weather.

"Yes." She watched him drink down half the bottle. "We're at fourteen inches and counting. City's declared a state of emergency, along with Baltimore, New York, and Boston. Nobody was spared with this storm. It's already being touted as the superstorm of the century."

"Hmph. Seems like there's a new one of those every year."

"You're telling me, but this one's definitely a record breaker. I called the office, and they don't want anyone attempting to come in until the roads are cleared, so I'm going to do what I can from here."

"All right. You can use Vaughn's computer. I'll try to stay out of your way."

With a nod, she straightened from the door jamb, then hesitated before turning to leave. "Cam?" She tried to hide it, but a sad kind of fear clouded her eyes. "Are we okay? Still friends?"

He thought of that little girl, and his heart broke all over again. So many people had let her down. He'd be damned before he was one of them. "Yeah, Eva. Always."

After the strange morning, Eva feared the rest of the day would have the same Alice-down-the-rabbit-hole feel. But Cam's presence was more of a balm than anything else and, true to his word, he stayed out of her way for the rest of the afternoon and let her get caught up on the piles of paperwork she'd been neglecting. In fact, having him at his own computer in the living room while she slogged through the hated administrative work felt enough like when they'd been partners that she experienced a pang or two of nostalgia throughout the day.

Eventually, Cam did interrupt her for dinner and threw a frozen pizza in the oven. It was nice to bullshit with him over pizza and beer like they always used to, but as dinner wound down, his demeanor changed. Heat flared between them, gasoline tossed on a banked fire, and the hungry look on his face made her go wet with anticipation. He reached over the counter, gently closed the lid of her borrowed computer, then led her by the hand to his bedroom, where he completely rocked her world.

Again.

She really had to be careful, because she could get used to this routine.

The following morning, she woke up before him—big surprise—and checked outside. It had stopped snowing, but the road was still impassible. As long as the snow continued to hold off, she figured the roads would be mostly clear by the end of the day, and life in the city would return to normal by tomorrow.

Why wasn't she more relieved about that?

Sighing at herself, she turned away from the window and rummaged through the kitchen for breakfast. She found Honey Nut Cheerios in the cupboard and a nearly empty gallon of milk in the fridge with a good expiration date. Worked for her. She munched on a bowl of the cereal and wondered what she should do today. She'd completed all of her backed-up paperwork via remote access to the department's network, but couldn't stand the thought of idle hours. She'd go batshit crazy from cabin fever by noon. Finishing her cereal, she decided to go back over the case files she had with her and retrieved her bag from the loft. Her phone, left charging on the desk, buzzed as she passed and she paused to check the screen. If it was work or Shelby—

Nope. Preston.

She let it go to voice mail like his past six calls, grabbed her bag, and continued down the ladder. She told him she'd think about taking him back, but that didn't mean she had to talk to him while she was thinking, right?

Two hours later, Cam bolted out of his room as if he was in hot pursuit of a criminal, all but slamming into the wall opposite his door.

"What's the rush?"

He skidded to a halt when he spotted her at the kitchen island, and sheer relief passed over his face before he hid it.

"Oh. Hey." As casually as he could manage, he strolled to the coffee maker as if that had been his destination all along. "Mornin'."

Had he thought she left in the middle of the night again?

She winced at his back as shame washed over her. She should apologize for her cowardly actions in Key West, but… Damn, it was all so embarrassing now. She couldn't bring herself to voluntarily broach the topic with him.

"Good morning," she said instead.

"Sleep well?"

She snorted. "When you let me."

He turned with his mug in hand and gave a dimpled smile that would drop a nun's panties. "My work here is—no, on second thought, forget I said that. I'm nowhere near done with you yet."

She shook her head and tried to return to her files, but the sensual promise in his words had her heating up in all the best places. Her mind wandered to the memory of his hands on her skin, his mouth on her sex— "Whatcha working on?"

His question brought back her focus and guilt stung her. This particular file deserved all of her attention and since he walked into the room, it hadn't gotten any.

"The Dunphy-Adams case," she answered and flipped to the crime scene photos. If anything could douse her lust fast, it'd be those gruesome, graphic pictures. "It's finally going to trial and my court date is next week. I'm refreshing my memory on the details." Not that she really wanted to revisit the details—it had been one of those cases she'd rather not remember, but would probably never forget. Charles Dunphy had brutally killed Selena Adams, his eleven-year-old step-daughter, and although they had arrested Dunphy on some pretty solid evidence early on in the investigation, she'd always felt there were too many loose ends in the case. Mainly, his motive. There was no discernible reason Dunphy would want his step-daughter dead. Yet, she was, and his DNA was all over her and the knife used to kill her.

"Dunphy-Adams," Cam said and his eyes rolled toward the ceiling as he did a mental calculation. "That was…what? Three years ago? And it's just going to trial now?"

"The defense threw up as many road blocks as they could."

Cam moved around the end of the island and leaned over her shoulder to study the crime scene photos. "Yeah, I remember this case. It always bothered the hell out of me that we were never able to prove his brother's involvement."

"Me, too, and we still can't. Gordon Dunphy is never going to be charged unless his brother talks. And Charles hasn't talked to anyone but his lawyer for years." She slumped into her seat and rolled her head around on her neck in an effort to relieve the tightness in her back.

Cam's big hands settled on her shoulders, his thumbs digging into the worst knots along her spine, and she bit back a moan at the pleasure-pain of his strong fingers kneading out the tension.

"Is Gordon still causing problems?" he asked.

"If by that you mean he's still obnoxiously insisting his brother has been wrongfully accused? Hell, yes. But is he still attacking the lead investigators in bars? Not that I'm aware. I think he's mostly forgotten about us. Do you still have the restraining order against him?"

Cam's fingers stilled and she turned in her seat to look at him. "Do you?"

"No," he answered slowly. "I forgot about it until just now. I think it expired last month."

She studied him, instincts screaming he was holding something back from her, but she saw no evidence of it in his expression. Man had an unreadable poker face when he wanted to. "Have you had trouble with him since?"

"Nah. Like you said, he probably forgot about me. I'm no longer the threat to his brother's freedom—the court is." Dismissing the subject with a shrug, Cam resumed massaging her shoulders and pressed his lips lightly to the bare skin at the base of her neck. "I think you need a break. You're all tense."

God, it felt so good. His kneading fingers digging into her muscles, the kiss sending chills down her spine. She wanted more—his lips, his hands all over her. And, dammit, that was not a part of the deal they'd made. She moved out of his reach and shut the file on the Dunphy case.

"Cam, stop. You're touching me like…"

Confusion drew his brows together. "Like what?"

She sighed. "Like we're lovers."

"We are. Didn't we talk about this yesterday?"

"No, we're friends with benefits. Fuck buddies. There's a big difference between our arrangement and lovers."

He opened his mouth, but closed it again without speaking, and his lips thinned into a hard line. He backed up a step, hands raised. "You're right. Sorry. I got carried away."

She nodded and busied herself with gathering up the files she had spread across the counter. Of course she was right...

But then why did pushing him away feel so wrong?

"It's fine," she said. "I'm going to shower. It's stopped snowing and the roads should be clear by this afternoon."

If he was disappointed by that news, he didn't show it. "Oh. Good." He picked up his coffee, drank deeply.

Good? Was that all he had to say? "So, I'm going to go home and pick up a change of clothes, then check in at work, see if they need any help."

He circled the island, grabbed a bowl from the dishwasher, and poured himself some cereal. The lack of milk didn't deter him. "I'm sure you'll be busy this week."

She watched him dig in to the dry cereal, outrage stealing through her at his offhand tone. Was he *ready* to be rid of her?

Man, now she kind of wanted to punch him.

She stood. "Yes, I'm sure I will be."

"So...you probably wouldn't want to catch a movie Friday."

Her outrage softened into a warm glow that spread through her body. Then a horrible thought struck. "You're not asking me out on a date, are you? Because—"

"No! No, no. Aw, shit." He gave up on the cereal and set it aside. "I swear I didn't mean it to sound like that. You've drawn the line pretty damn clear between us, and I'm trying not to cross over it. But—" He stopped and rubbed his jaw, obviously at a loss for words. "Listen, I don't know how to talk to you now. Before, I'd just call you up and say, 'Hey, Thor 2's playing. Let's go get our geek on.' But now, feels like everything I say has a double meaning. An offer to see a movie, or grab a bite to eat, or go to Maguire's for a beer, sounds like I'm after a date."

Eva laughed and dropped back to her seat. "I know. I guess we have to come up with some rules for this friends with benefits thing."

He nodded and leaned toward her, flattening his palms on the counter. "Rule one: If I suggest we go to the movies, I'm not asking you on a date. Even if we end up in bed afterward, it's still not a date."

"Rule two," she said. "This isn't a permanent deal. If you find someone you'd like to pursue romantically, we're done. We go back to plain old friendship. We're not cheating on anyone with each other."

"Ah, good one." His dimple appeared again with his smile. "Should we be writing these down?"

"Smart ass." She gave him a playful shove, then stood. "I'm gonna shower."

"Wait, I have another rule," he called after her. "Three: Showers are always better together."

"Nice try, Wilde." Walking backwards to see his reaction, she added, "And, yes, I want to get my geek on Friday if it involves Chris Hemsworth. He's *numero uno* on my freebie list."

Cam's eyes narrowed. "Your freebie list?"

"Yeah. If he walked through the door right now and wanted to jump in the shower with me, it's a freebie. Not considered cheating." She looked at the front door expectantly and waited several seconds before snapping her fingers. "Damn. Guess it's not happening today. A girl can dream."

Cam pushed away from the counter and, scowling, prowled toward her. "Lemme get this straight. You'd shower with Thor—"

"In a heartbeat."

"—but I'm not allowed."

"I had no idea you were into tall, blond, and built Aussies, too." Biting the inside of her cheek to keep from laughing, she spun away and continued to the bathroom. "That could be kinda hot, but I think your shower is too small for the three of us."

She made it to the bathroom before he trapped her against the door with his heavy weight. A thrill zinged straight to her libido as his teeth caught the sensitive spot at the nape of her neck and pulled with a little, punishing tug. Goose bumps raced along her skin and her nipples pebbled, aching for the heat of his mouth. Against her back, his cock hardened and lengthened, and she went damp with anticipation.

She chuckled. "Are you jealous of my freebie list? That breaks one of the rules of friends with benefits. No jealousy."

"Nah." His hot breath whispered over her ear. "I just wanted an excuse to get you naked in the shower again."

"But that's the best thing about friends with benefits." She turned in the circle of his arms and wound hers around his neck. "You never need an excuse."

Chapter Sixteen

Could the week go any fucking slower?

As the city dug out from under nearly three feet of snow, Cam held down the Wilde Security office. Vaughn was out chasing leads for his missing person case, Reece had traveled up to Philly to install a home security system as soon as the roads cleared, and Jude was still on his honeymoon. And Greer — well, who the fuck knew where he was? The way he'd been ghosting around lately, he could be on Mars for all Cam knew.

On Tuesday morning, Cam tracked down Arnold Mabry and found out from the man's parole officer that he lived in a group home for parolees and worked as an overnight stocker at the local Wal-Mart. That night, Cam went grocery shopping. He spent some time watching Mabry work and even approached him with a question about a product that was missing from the shelves. Guy was relaxed and friendly enough in that customer-is-always-right way. No nervousness and not even a flicker of recognition.

Whoever hired Soup to kill Cam, it wasn't Mabry.

Strike one.

On Wednesday, a fed-up housewife came into the office wanting to catch her hubby in the act with his mistress. Cam didn't much care for the woman—she was shrill and demanding and he, frankly, could see why the husband stepped out on her. He'd only spent an hour with her and ended up nursing a pounding headache by the time she left. But he took on the case because cheating spouses were Wilde Security's bread and butter, and he was having zero luck tracking down Tom Lindquist, who never checked in with his parole officer and was in the wind.

At first, Cam had enjoyed the peace and quiet around the office as he worked on the case of the browbeaten cheater and his very own felon version of Where's Waldo with Lindquist. It was kinda nice not having to play referee between his brothers. And, since they weren't here, he didn't have to worry about some hitman coming into the office and opening fire on them in an attempt to get to him, which had been a growing concern of his since the storm ended. He'd found himself getting increasingly more paranoid whenever he was around them, checking and double checking doors and windows, making sure he wasn't followed to the office or back home. So, the week of solitude was a pleasant respite.

For a while.

Now, though, he fidgeted with a bad case of cabin fever. Funny—during the storm, he hadn't gotten restless. But he'd had Eva to keep him company.

Eva.

He smiled and considered calling her, but a glance at the

clock in the corner of his computer screen stayed his hand. She was probably still busy in court with the Dunphy case. Besides, she'd already sent him a text saying she couldn't wait for their non-date tomorrow, because the whole police force had been pulling double-duty since the storm ended and she was in need of some downtime.

Ah, the glamorous life of a civil servant. A small, nostalgic part of him missed those days. But the rest of him told that part to fuck off. Private investigation was a good gig that paid better and had much better hours.

And long stretches of boredom. Like today.

By mid-day, Cam had played at least twenty rounds of Spider Solitaire on the computer, caught up on all the football and hockey game highlights he'd missed, and gotten his fill of Facebook—although, had to admit, it still amused the hell out of him every time he saw the meme featuring Jude in his underwear carrying a giant iguana. A tourist had taken the photo in Key West over summer, uploaded it to Reddit, and it had gone viral. Now, it was a mainstay in the strange online world of meme-dom.

And, lookie, here's one he hadn't seen before.

Cam sent it to the printer and taped it to what had fondly been named The Wall of Internet Shame behind Jude's desk.

Hah. Little bro was going to love that one.

On his way back to his own desk, he stopped by the office fridge to snag a bottle of water and considered closing up shop for the day. It was foolish to sit around here doing nothing on the off-chance that someone would stop in with a job. He could be out tailing the cheater, which was about as mind-numbing as staring at Facebook all day, but at least he'd be out of the office.

No doubt Reece would have a fit if he closed early.

Decisions, decisions.

Just as Cam sat down and twisted off the cap of his water, the front door opened and Greer stalked in, bringing a bad mood and the chill of winter in his wake.

"Cam, my office."

Cam winced, recapped the bottle of water, and set it aside before pushing away from his desk. Greer was using his Army Ranger tone again, which meant hop-to or face his wrath. Still, Cam took the time to lock the front door before heading back, and Greer was already seated behind a disaster area of a desk when he dropped into one of the visitor's chairs.

"What's up?"

"Have you validated the information from your informant yet?" Greer asked.

"Uh, no." He'd been dreading this convo, but managed to keep his wince inward. "About that. My informant died of a drug overdose last weekend before the storm. I have no way of verifying what he said."

Yeah, it was a lie—that five hundred dollars in Soup's pocket had pretty much put to rest any doubts he had about the validity of the information. Someone had given Soup that money and he'd most likely died because he took the down payment but didn't do what he'd been paid for.

The contract on Cam's head was real.

But this was one case he was going to handle on his own. It was too dangerous, and he wouldn't risk any of his brothers getting hurt for him.

Greer didn't explode like Cam had expected. Actually, he looked too tired to get angry about anything. Probably why he simply nodded in response. "So do you know of anyone who wants you dead?"

Cam lounged back in the creaky wood chair. "I already told you, the list is long and varied."

And had recently grown by one with Eva's news about the Dunphy-Adams case finally going to trial. He'd forgotten about Gordon Dunphy, but the guy, as a fairly well-off real estate broker, fit the vague description of the man who offered Soup a thousand dollars for Cam's life.

Although, Cam had no clue why Gordon would want him dead when he no longer had any influence over the case. Hell, maybe Gordon was just a champion grudge holder. Something worth checking into later—but not something his brothers needed to worry about.

Greer eyed him over a stack of papers. "You're not too concerned about any of this."

"No. As I said before, it's probably nothing. Soup used to be a good informant, but his reliability has slipped over the last few years as the drugs took over his life. I would not be surprised if he made it all up to squeeze me for money." Cam leaned forward and rested his elbows on his knees. "And, honestly, I'm more worried about you. You could drive a semi though those bags under your eyes. Tell me the truth, have you been sleeping?"

Greer waved a dismissive hand. "Couple hours a night."

"That's not enough."

"I've survived on less."

"I don't doubt that. But, here's the thing, bro. You don't *have* to survive on less. So, wanna tell me what's going on?"

"Nothing. I'm good."

"And I'm Iron Man. Seriously, Greer."

Greer spun his chair toward the little window on the wall behind him, which overlooked the small fenced-in dog park of his apartment complex across the way. A woman stood bundled against the cold as her golden retriever romped through the snow drifts, and Greer focused intently on the two of them.

All right. Cam knew a dismissal when he saw one. He stood, but couldn't make himself leave. "You ever need to talk, I'll listen." He got half way to the door before Greer spoke again.

"Nightmares."

Damn. Cam paused and glanced back. His brother hadn't moved, still watched the woman and her dog playing like his life depended on keeping them in his sight. "What kind?"

"Just...nightmares. They'll go away. Always do." He cleared his throat and turned away from the window, but only slightly. "Go get some legwork done on the cheating husband case. I'll close up here."

Cam left his brother's office with a knot in his gut. Grabbed his jacket and cell phone from his desk and waited until he was in the 4Runner before dialing a number he'd gotten in Key West.

Seth Harlan answered after a half dozen rings, sounding wary. "Hello?"

"Hey, it's Cam Wilde."

"Cam?" The wariness evaporated into surprise. "Oh. Hi. Uh, what can I do for you?"

"I have a question and it's kinda personal, but I'm worried about someone, and I need to know the answer."

A beat of silence came from the other end, and he imagined Seth mentally fortifying himself.

"Okay, I'm ready. Go ahead."

"How did your PTSD first present itself?"

Seth sucked in a breath. "Nightmares," he said on the exhale. "About a week after I woke up in the hospital, I started having nightmares."

"Shit. That's what I was afraid you'd say." Except something wasn't ringing true here. "You said it started about a week after you regained consciousness? Is that a normal time span for the on-set of symptoms?"

"Yeah. Symptoms can appear anytime from right after the traumatic event up to three months later."

"But not years later."

"Not usually," Seth answered. "No."

Cam stared at the front of the Wilde Security office, an acidic pit opening up in his stomach. Greer had been out of the military for a long time. Too long to just now be experiencing the symptoms of PTSD…so what the fuck was going on?

"It's your oldest brother you're worried about, isn't it?" Seth asked softly.

Surprise rippled through Cam, and he returned his full attention to the phone. "How'd you know?"

"I saw it in him at Jude's wedding. He was jumpy, crowd made him nervous. At first I thought I was projecting, but…" He paused. "If you want to give me his number, I can talk to him. Dunno how much good I'll do because I'm a head case myself, but maybe I can help."

"Thanks. I owe you one."

Seth made a sound that might have been a laugh. "You Wildes are all the same. You don't owe me shit."

A Kit Kat bar sat on Eva's desk when she returned from a disastrous day in court. Christ, did she ever need the chocolate pick-me-up. The judge had declared a key piece of evidence inadmissible, which made her testimony irrelevant and was going to seriously hurt the prosecution's case against Charles Dunphy.

The memory of his brother Gordon's smug smile as she exited the courtroom still made her blood run cold.

Eva unwrapped the candy, broke off a piece, and searched for Cam. He was the only one who ever dropped chocolate on her desk, so he had to be here...

She spotted him talking to a few other detectives over by the coffee maker and waved. He caught her gaze and smiled faintly, then excused himself from the conversation.

"Thanks for the chocolate," she said as he approached and bit into a piece.

"Figured you'd need it. I heard about what happened in court today."

"Sheesh. Good news travels," she said, heavy on the sarcasm, and took another bite of her candy.

Cam nodded. "Nothing faster. I know we have plans for tomorrow, but want to grab a bite and talk it over?"

She started to decline. With how backed up the department was because of the storm, she should decline. But he seemed...worried. Or something. Besides, she was off for the night, and the idea of spending time with Cam sent a thrill jittering around her belly.

"Sure, but you're buying." She broke off another stick from her Kit Kat and pointed it at him. He leaned forward and bit it out of her hand, which so should not have lit her up with all kinds of erotic fantasies. Heat shot straight between her thighs and she looked around, afraid that somehow, someone had noticed her sudden arousal. She was in a room full of detectives, after all, but the only person the least bit interested in the flush riding her cheeks was Cam. He grinned and slung an arm over her shoulders, all buddy-buddy like, but the warmth radiating from him only amped up her desire.

They made it as far as the parking lot.

Cam crushed her up against his SUV's door, and his mouth descended, hot and demanding, full of erotic temptation. The heat she'd felt with his embrace inside was nothing like the inferno that engulfed her now, and the freezing wind whipping her hair around her head went unnoticed. She clutched his shoulders, dragging him in tighter, needing him closer.

He grinned into the kiss. "Demanding."

"Horny," she corrected.

He patted her ass. "Maybe we can do something about that later."

Later?

Christ, she was so hot, she was surprised her skin wasn't steaming right now.

Cam laughed and backed away. In his absence, the cold air slapped some sense into her and she straightened her twisted coat, scanning the parking lot to make sure nobody saw that moment of indiscretion with her best friend. She must be losing her ever-loving mind.

Cam nudged her aside, then opened the car door for her. She wanted to kick him for it. Her feelings must have been broadcasted loud and clear in her expression because his grin only widened, and he added a quick bow and a murmured, "My lady," before shutting the door.

She punched his bicep when he climbed into the driver's side. "You're such an asshat."

"You wouldn't want me any other way."

Grumbling, she slouched into the seat and watched the passing streets. Sad truth was, he'd hit the nail on the head. She didn't want him any other way…

Well, except maybe naked.

She studied him from the corner of her eye, noting the strain at the front of his jeans. She let her fingers follow her gaze, trailing them lightly over the bulge.

Cam sucked in a sharp breath.

Yeah, naked would be really good. She made short work of his button, slid down his zipper, and freed his cock. He growled as she stroked him, helpless to do anything because he had to keep his hands on the wheel and eyes on the road. For once, he was completely in her control. She liked it.

"Eva," he groaned.

"Betcha can't make it until we get to Maguire's."

"You're evil."

"Nope. Told you, just horny."

"What do I get if I make it?"

She licked her lips and leaned over the center console. "Me."

Cam hit the gas, taking every shortcut he knew. Maguire's wasn't far from the police department, but with heaps of snow blocking some roads, the trip took twice as long. He whipped into the parking lot as the light suction of her mouth sent every muscle in his body into spasms. At six-thirty at night, the lot was mostly empty, and he parked as far back as possible, tucked in the shadow of a dark office building. He left the SUV running, but switched off the lights and shoved his seat back. Eva was already a step ahead of him, shimmying out of her pants, pulling aside her panties, and straddling his lap.

The first penetration made them both groan. Perfect. He had the oddest sense of coming home.

Then she fused her mouth over his and he held her hips steady as he pumped into her, the sex fast and dirty, more about release than connection. When she came, her body clamped down so hard, she squeezed his release from him.

Eva collapsed forward, her forehead resting on his shoulder as she trembled through the aftershocks. "Whew. I've been wanting to do that all week."

"Me, too." He raised a hand to stroke her hair and back, but caught himself. Friends with benefits. Not lovers. Right. To cover his gaffe, he instead ran his fingers through his own hair. "Why didn't you call?"

Lifting her head, she smiled down at him. "I thought about it. More than once, but everything has been so crazy since the storm…" She trailed off and bit her lower lip in a way that was both vulnerable and insanely sexy. "I missed you, though."

Throat suddenly thick with emotion, Cam nodded. "Same here."

A buzzing phone broke the spell of cozy afterglow, and Eva winced. "Damn. Sometimes I hate technology."

Cam had to agree, especially when she lifted herself off him and the slide of her slick, sensitized flesh hardened him for a round two. She scrambled into the passenger seat and searched through her pants pockets until she found the ringing phone.

She scowled. "Preston."

The guy's name registered like a punch. *Keep cool. Don't let her see it.* "Does he call a lot?"

"Lately, yeah." She replaced the phone in her pocket and slid her pants up her legs, lifting her ass off the seat to button them. "He says he wants a second chance."

Cam's stomach dropped into his pelvic cradle. Well, that deflated his hopes of a repeat. He tucked himself in and zipped his jeans. This was a conversation better had while dressed. And, possibly, drunk. "Let's go inside."

Cam waited until they settled at the bar and had their drinks before asking, "You're not going to give in, are you?"

"I don't know."

Friends with benefits, he reminded himself when he discovered his hand tightening on his glass. Not lovers. He had no say whatsoever in who she dated. Goddammit. "How can you not know?"

"I just…" She traced the rim of her glass with one finger. "You remember me telling you the kind of life I want for any kids I have? The perfect sitcom family? Preston fits that mold."

And Cam didn't.

He took a swig of his beer to ease the tightness in his throat. He couldn't be mad at her, but that didn't stop him from feeling the sting of her rejection right down to his core. He was good enough for sex. Good enough to be her best friend. But not good enough to be a husband to her, a father to those future kids she so badly wanted. And fuck if it wasn't his own fault. How many times had he told her over the years, whenever she tried to set him up with someone, that he wasn't looking for marriage?

Obviously, enough times that she'd taken it to heart.

But who was he kidding? He didn't believe in the kind of idyllic life she dreamed about and couldn't give it to her. Even the idea of attempting it left him cold with a bone-deep kind of terror.

But, damn. *Preston?*

"You can do better," he told her.

Her sigh moved her shoulders. "I tell myself that, too, but what if I can't?"

Christ, her mother had done a number on her self-esteem. "Eva, listen to me. Preston is no good for you. Not only can you do better, but you deserve better."

"You're only saying that 'cause you hate him."

"Yeah, but it's also the truth." He hesitated, and his next words felt like shards of glass ripping up his throat. "Some-day, you'll find the guy who's perfect for you, who'll give you that family you've always wanted."

"Can we not talk about this?" She lifted her beer, in-dicating him with a tilt of the glass. "How about we discuss why you looked so worried earlier?"

No. As much as he trusted her, he didn't feel comfortable airing out Greer's problems in front of her. "How about we talk about the Dunphy case?"

"Ah, murder. What does it say about us that we find it easier than personal shit?"

He worked up a smile and tapped his glass to hers. "That we're two peas from the same very fucked-up pod."

"Amen to that."

Chapter Seventeen

A rusted out pick-up truck sat in the driveway where Eva normally parked when she got home around eleven-thirty that night. After the amazing car sex and awkward personal conversation, she and Cam had commiserated over the failed Dunphy case, then settled into their usual routine of friendly bickering, which ended in a competitive game of darts. She'd won, of course. Someday, he'd learn not to bet against her when it came to darts—but until that day came, she'd have fun taking his twenty bucks.

By the time he dropped her by her car in the police station's lot, every ounce of stress had seeped out of her spine, leaving her damn close to school girl giddy. They had decided to keep their plans for tomorrow night to go see *Thor 2* and already, she couldn't wait.

But the tension returned, clamping a vice grip around her spine as she parked her car next to the unfamiliar truck and got out. Maryland plates. The color used to be green as far as she could tell, but a combination of age and neglect had faded it out to the same muddy brown of the Potomac after a storm. Debris filled the bed and a quick peek through the window showed piles of fast food wrappers and beer cans littering the cab.

Music blasted from her house so loud that the base thudded in her chest.

Dammit. She was going to kick her sister's ass.

Fuming, Eva strode through the gate and up the steps, throwing open the front door hard enough to rattle the windows—if they weren't already vibrating from the music. A skinny guy with a shock of greasy dreadlocks lay passed out on her couch, an open beer resting on his concave stomach and a joint burning down in his limp hand. The scent of pot filled the air in a cloyingly sweet cloud, and she started throwing open windows, heating bill be damned.

Pausing at the foot of the couch, she didn't dare touch the guy to wake him. He looked—and smelled—as if he hadn't bathed in months. But she did take the beer before it spilled and picked the joint out of his fingers because he was seconds from dropping it.

What the hell? This guy was not Shelby's usual type. Yes, she vacillated wildly when it came to the men she'd dated, but they always fell somewhere on the scale between uber-geek hipster and punk rocker. Never drugged-out hippy. That was more like—

Oh, God.

Horror skittered across her skin as a slim figure appeared under the archway that separated kitchen from living room, and her worst fears came crashing into her home in the form of a woman-child who never understood the meaning of motherhood.

"Mom?"

"Honey!" Katrina breezed through the living room and pecked an air kiss on each of Eva's cheeks. "So glad you're home. I see you've already started without me." She winked and hip-checked Eva hard enough to spill the beer she hadn't set down yet. "At least one of my girls knows how to have a good time. Shel-Bear is being a party pooper."

Eva looked toward the kitchen. Shelby hung back and lifted her shoulders in a helpless shrug when Eva met her gaze with a question in her own. Yeah, thanks, Shelby. A lot of help she was.

Eva set down the beer and dropped the joint into the can. "Mom, who is that guy?"

"That's Doug. We've been living together in Baltimore." She lowered her voice and leaned in as if to divulge a state secret. "He's perfectly wonderful."

"Yeah. Looks like Prince Charming."

"Eee-va," Katrina drew her name out on a whine. "Don't be bitchy. You should be happy for your mama. I think I've finally found The One."

"You said the same thing about my father. And Shel's. And about Tony, the loan shark. Shane, the car thief. Jamal, the drug dealer. Oh, and who could forget Evander, the stripper? Or Aaron, doing time for double homicide?"

"Aaron was innocent."

"Mom, he was caught with blood literally on his hands!"

"Well, this time it's different. Doug and I are in love."

Yeah, like Eva hadn't heard that before. A headache began pounding in beat with the music, and she found the source—an actual boombox, straight out of the nineties, tape deck and everything. She yanked the cord out of the wall and Doug the One woke with a sputtered, "Hey!" Then after glancing around with droopy eyes, he added, "Where the fuck's my joint?"

Uh-huh. Definitely another winner.

She faced her mother again. "What are you doing here? Why aren't you still in Baltimore?"

Katrina instantly bristled. "What, I can't come visit my girls?"

"Mom."

"Oh, all right." She flapped her skinny arms and sighed like answering the question was somehow a huge favor. "We got evicted. But it wasn't our fault! The fucking landlord…"

Something else Eva had heard before. Nothing was ever Katrina's fault, and the world was out to get her, and blah, blah, blah.

Christ almighty, Eva was sick of it. Closing her eyes, she pinched the bridge of her nose and focused on breathing until Katrina wound down the rant. Except, she was just getting started, and after about five minutes of increasingly frenetic and paranoid claims, Eva couldn't take it anymore.

"Mom. Mom. Mom!"

Panting, wild eyed, Katrina spun on her. "What?"

"You can't stay here."

"Why not? Don't you love me anymore?" Like that, her fanatical expression crumpled into a pout, and Eva caved. This was her mother, after all.

"All right, *you* can stay, but not that guy. I'm not supporting one of your deadbeat boyfriends."

Katrina's gaze cut to her one true love and tears welled in her blue eyes. "Eva, honey, you can't possibly expect me to choose between my daughters and the man I love."

Yes, she absolutely could. On this point, the pout wasn't going to sway her. She stood her ground as tears trickled prettily down her mother's cheeks.

"I can't leave him."

Eva nodded and only felt the tiniest pinch of regret. She'd been down this road one too many times to feel more than that. "Then you need to find someplace else to go."

"We'll freeze out there."

Shelby, who had ghosted in from the kitchen, spoke up. "What about that place I told you about? I already called them and they'll take you in. They'll take you both." There was so much hope in Shelby's eyes and voice, so much longing for a relationship with their mother, and Eva's heart ripped in two when Katrina whirled and spat in Shelby's direction.

"You ungrateful little bitch. You want to lock me up and throw away the key."

"No!" Shelby protested. "Mom, I swear, that's not what I want. But this place...they'll help you get off the drugs and—"

Katrina launched across the space separating them and slammed her fist so hard into Shelby's face, they both staggered backwards.

Eva froze, staring in stunned horror at the woman who had birthed her. For all of their mother's faults, she'd always protected them, never once raised a finger to intentionally hurt either of them. But now here she was, screaming nonsense, tearing at Shelby's hair, raking her nails across Shelby's face, and trying to freaking *bite* her daughter. Doug howled with a maniac kind of laughter from the couch.

Holy fuck.

Eva grabbed her handcuffs from her belt under her jacket and flattened her mother out with a tackle. Sobbing, Shelby scrambled away from Katrina's still clawing hands until her back pressed against the wall.

Katrina had more strength in her five-foot, ninety-eight pound body than Eva anticipated and broke free, only to meet with the business end of Shelby's Doc Martens. The kick stunned her long enough for Eva to yank her hands behind her back and slap the cuffs around her wrists.

"Call the police," she ordered Shelby.

At those words, Doug stopped laughing. His eyes widened, and he dove for the front door. A second later, his truck sputtered to life.

Too bad for him, Eva had his plate number.

After dropping Eva off at her car, Cam went home, but found he couldn't settle and decided to make a quick trip to the office to grab some papers on the browbeaten cheater case. He'd gathered enough evidence that his client should have no trouble making a solid case for divorce, but he wanted to put it all together in a presentable report before he met with her again tomorrow. So he threw on his coat and trekked back out into the cold.

Reece's Escalade sat in the Wilde Security lot—he must have retired his sports cars until spring—and the lights blazed from behind the front door as Cam used his key to get in. Damn. He'd hoped none of his brothers would be here this time of night. And he hadn't been as careful about

checking his surroundings since he and Eva left for Maguire's, too distracted by sex and her call from Preston to worry
about the hitman lurking somewhere in the city, waiting for
a shot at him. But that worry came roaring back now. He set
a hand on his gun under his coat and scanned the parking
lot. Nothing moved, no cars drove by on the street.

Jesus. If the hitman didn't get to him, this creeping sense
of paranoia would.

Exhaling with relief, he pushed through the door. Reece stood by the coffee pot, waiting for it to finish brew-
ing, his tie loosened and his shirt sleeves rolled up to his elbows, which was about as relaxed as the second oldest Wilde
brother ever got. The only sounds in the office were the bub-
bling of the coffee as it percolated and the police scanner,
a low static hum in the background. Cam hated having the
thing on, because the cop in him couldn't tune it out like his
brothers could.

"Hey, bro," Cam said and locked the door again before
he crossed to his desk. "Didn't know you'd be back tonight."

Reece glanced over his shoulder as he poured himself
a mug from the fresh pot, his eyes red-rimmed. "You're in a
disgustingly good mood for midnight."

Okay, yeah, there was a distinct bounce in his step, but
hot car sex did that to a guy. "Eh, I'm a night owl. How was
Philly?"

"A headache."

"Then why aren't you home?"

"Because I picked up three more home security jobs
while there, and I have to put together option packages for
each."

Why that was so urgent it couldn't wait until tomorrow,

Cam had no idea, but he didn't bother arguing. When it came to business or computers, Reece was a machine. Hell, the guy was a freaking Terminator and people in the city quaked at the thought of ending up on the wrong side of a boardroom table from him. Before Greer brought him in on the idea of starting Wilde Security, Reece had founded a corporation that created computer simulations for military use, and he held the kinds of security clearances that most people had no clue even existed. He had more money than he could spend in two lifetimes, and Cam often suspected it was his sole financial support that kept Wilde Security afloat.

So, yeah, not a guy to argue with when it came to work.

Cam gathered what he needed from his desk, then headed toward the door. "Don't work too hard."

"Cam."

Shit. That tone didn't bode well for the coming conversation. Maybe he could still escape and preserve his good mood for a little while longer. He eyed the door, but decided against making a run for it. Wilde men didn't run.

He blew out a breath and faced his brother. "If you're gonna start in on me about the supposed contract that's on my head, don't. I already talked to Greer about it."

"Yes, I know. And then you turned the conversation to Greer's problems."

"Rightfully so. Have you looked at him lately? There's something fucked up going on with him."

"I'm aware." Reece perched on the edge of Jude's desk and crossed his feet at the ankles. Several beats of silence slipped by as he sipped his coffee.

"And…?" Cam prompted.

"And Greer's not the issue right now. We need to focus

on this problem of yours first."

Jesus Christ. Why wouldn't his brothers get off his back about this? He had it handled, and for their own sakes, they didn't need to be involved. "It's not a problem, Reece. Nothing has happened to me. Nothing is going to happen to me. I'm telling you, this whole thing about a hit was just Soup's way of prying money out of me. So, drop it."

Reece heaved a sigh. "You know, you have a really bad habit of deflecting—"

Cam held up a hand as buzz from the scanner caught his attention. Domestic dispute between a mother and her daughters. Drugs possibly involved. Injuries reported. A detective already at the scene...

Reece's eyes narrowed. "Isn't that—"

"Eva's house. Fuck." As his heart lodged like a rock in his throat, he dropped the files he was holding and bolted for the door, but Reece caught his arm.

"Whoa, I'll drive. You work on getting a hold of Eva."

Chapter Eighteen

As Reece hit the highway breaking every speed limit, Cam's phone buzzed in his pocket. Eva's name appeared on the display, and he snapped it up, air exploding out of his lungs in relief that she'd returned his frantic calls.

"Are you okay?"

She drew a breath that shook. "Mom attacked Shelby."

"I know. I heard it on the scanner. Are *you* okay?"

Silence.

His heart damn near stopped. "Baby, answer me."

"Cam." Her voice broke on his name. "I need you."

"I'm on my way." He thumped the dashboard with his palm. Reece all but stood on the gas, and twenty frustrating minutes later, they were pulling up behind a swarm of police vehicles.

Apparently, he wasn't the only one who recognized her address.

His feet hit the pavement before Reece had the Escalade

in park. Several of the officers recognized him and pointed to the ambulance backed ass-end to the curb in front of Eva's house, but when he looked inside, he found two paramedics talking sedately over a petite blond woman. Strapped down to the gurney, she was out cold.

Eva's mother.

It was the first look he'd ever gotten of the woman, and he saw little resemblance between Katrina Bremer and Eva. Wherever Eva was dark—hair, skin, eyes—Katrina was light. Why that relived him, he couldn't begin to guess.

One of the medics noticed him standing there and nodded toward the house. "Cardoso's inside. She and her sister are okay."

"Thanks." Without another thought for the woman who had brought Eva into the world, he spirited across the yard and up the steps. Reece met him at the door and followed him into the house.

First thing he noticed was the scent of pot clinging to the air. The second was Eva, standing at the kitchen counter with her back to him, pressing a bag of frozen peas to her sister's swollen eye. He wanted to cross the space and sweep her into his arms and got half way to her before remembering himself.

Friends.

She'd called him as her best friend, not her lover.

He slowed his pace and drew in several calming breaths before speaking. Just seeing her unharmed and in one piece would have to be enough. At least until he got her alone. "Is everyone okay?"

Eva spun and lurched forward a step like she wanted to throw herself into his embrace as much as he wanted to scoop her up and hold her. He even spread his arms to catch her, but she stopped short, and her cheeks filled with color as her gaze darted around the room. He tried to tell her with his eyes that nobody would blame her for breaking down, for leaning on him for comfort, but she only straightened her shoulders and answered his question.

"Shelby has a good shiner, but otherwise, we're both fine. Mom's going to the hospital for a psychiatric evaluation. We're pressing charges."

"No, we're not," Shelby said and jumped down from her seat on the counter. She moved around Eva, giving her sister a look with her one good eye that dared her to argue, then studied Cam for a moment before her gaze landed on Reece. "Whoa. Hey, Evie, look. It's Suit and Tie." She grinned and elbowed her sister. "Remember the hot guy from the coffee shop I told ya about? The one that eye-fucks me?"

Cam stared at his brother. "What the fuck? You hit on Eva's sister?"

"Not in words," Shelby said, still grinning. "He just always looks like he wants to lick me from head to toe. Like ice cream."

Eva bit her lower lip, but her laugh escaped in a snort, which set Shelby off until the two were all but rolling around on the floor in a fit of hysterical laughter.

Reece held up his hands and backed away. "Cam, I swear, I didn't touch her."

"And you're not going to. Eva's little sister? Bro, really?"

"Slurrrp," Shelby said between laughing gasps for air.

Reece shut his eyes. "I'm leaving. I imagine you're staying here tonight?"

"Yeah," Cam said. "I am."

"Right. Okay." He actually stumbled over himself backing away, like he couldn't get out of the house fast enough. "I have work to do."

Sometime after Reece's hasty exit and before the cops left, Shelby's laughing fit devolved into shuddering, gut-wrenching sobs. Cam watched with a horrible sense of helplessness as Eva tried to calm her. The medic said she was in shock, and she should go to the hospital, but Shelby had made her position on that idea quite clear earlier in the night, and Eva upheld her wish to stay home.

Eventually, the medic gave her a painkiller laced with a light sedative, and she finally drifted to sleep on the couch with her sister cradling her head.

"She's out," Eva said, her own exhaustion weighing heavy in her voice. She stroked a hand over Shelby's pink-streaked blond hair. "I haven't seen her cry like that in years. This really shook her up."

Had shaken Eva, too, although Cam didn't point it out. He pushed up from the chair he'd settled into. "Want me to carry her to her room?"

"Would you? I think she'll feel safer in her own bed." She glanced around the living room, wincing at the mess her mother had left. "And I want to clean up before she wakes. She doesn't need the visual reminder."

Cam nodded and very gently slid his arms underneath Shelby. The girl weighed next to nothing, and a fierce surge of protectiveness swamped him as he picked her up. Eva, he never much worried about because she could hold her own against anyone. It was one of the things he found so freaking sexy about her. But Shelby? As tiny as she was, she couldn't win a battle against a cockroach. And if anything ever happened to her, Eva would never recover from the heartbreak.

He would not let that happen.

"I got you, Shel," he murmured when he laid her down and she stirred restlessly. He pulled the covers over her and stood there, talking in soft tones until she settled again. He backed out and shut the door, listening for a moment to make sure she didn't wake.

Silence.

Good.

In the living room, he found Eva stuffing beer cans into a black garbage bag. Outwardly, she seemed to be holding it together well, but her movements were stiff, jerky, and each breath she exhaled came out a bit too ragged.

He crossed the room and wrapped his arms around her, wishing he could take the pain away. She stiffened for a moment, but then relaxed with a shudder and turned to bury her face in the crook of his neck. He stroked her back, trembles of suppressed emotion rippling underneath his hand. He wanted to tell her to let go, cry it out, but that would be as useless as yelling into a hurricane.

Sometimes he wished his woman wasn't quite so strong.

"Mom never physically abused us," she said eventually.

"I know."

"She was ranting, paranoid."

"Drugs do that to people."

"She's never going to change." She sighed. "I need to finish cleaning." But she stayed put, clinging to him like she couldn't bear to let him go.

"Leave it for the morning," he whispered into her hair. "Let's go to bed."

She didn't protest. Just went to show how emotionally wiped out she was. He scooped her into his arms. She wasn't as light as Shelby. He didn't want her to be. He wanted a woman who wouldn't feel like porcelain in his hands, with the strength to stand up to him in bed and out, and he loved Eva's body, all long, sleek muscle with soft curves in exactly the right places.

His cock hardened and he mentally cursed himself for it. Not tonight. Tonight was about comfort. Tonight, he'd be the friend she needed.

As he set her on the edge of her bed, she grabbed a fistful of his shirt and dragged his mouth to hers. A branding kiss. Claiming. Her hands slid down his chest to the waistband of his pants, and she tugged him forward. He followed her onto the mattress, but switched their positions so that she was on top, letting her take the lead this time, set the pace. She shoved at his shirt; he lifted his head so she could get it off, and her mouth found his nipple. The hot, insistent tug made his cock jump, pinching him against the front of his jeans. It was the best kind of pain, and he groaned as her mouth trailed down. She undid his fly with her lips and teeth, kissed her way down his straining erection through the cotton of his boxer-briefs.

He knotted his hands in the sheet under him, curtailing the urge to touch her, to get her under him and taste her sweet pussy before he took her.

This was her show. Whatever she wanted.

She released his cock and her mouth engulfed him, her

tongue tracing the underside until his hips bucked off the bed of their own accord. She made a pleased humming noise in her throat that traveled up his shaft and nailed him in the gut.

Christ, he wanted inside her.

Eva swirled her tongue over his head one last time before her mouth left him and she dragged his pants off. She made short work of her own clothing, and her skin was cool against his as she slid up his overheated body, her mouth blazing a hot trail along his flesh.

By the time she straddled him and accepted him deep into her body, he trembled with need. She moved slow, raising herself over him, her fingers trailing down her stomach to find them where they were joined. She rubbed her own clit and so many dirty thoughts tumbled through his mind, but he bit them back. There was a time for that kind of talk, and now wasn't it.

But, fuck, she was driving him insane.

He allowed his hands to uncurl from the sheet and move to her thighs, then to her ass. But he didn't urge her to quicken the pace, didn't hold her still and pump into her like he wanted. He watched her take pleasure in his body and her own, and the sight was the most erotic thing he'd ever seen in his life. Her head fell back, spilling her dark hair down her back. A moan vibrated from her throat as her thighs tightened around his hips and she moved faster, her breasts bouncing, her moans sharpening into little cries until a hard spasm quaked through her and he lost all sense of sight as his own orgasm rocketed from him.

Gasping, she collapsed on his chest. He released his grip on her ass and slid his hands up her back, down again, up, down.

She let loose with a shuddering sound that was as close to a sob as he'd ever heard from her. He wrapped her up in his arms, rolling so that they lay side by side, their bodies still locked together in the most intimate of ways.

Her heavy-lidded eyes opened and searched his face. "How can you do that?" she whispered. "Give up control so easily like that?"

"Sweetheart, it isn't about control. Never was."

"You like being in control."

"I do," he admitted and swept a strand of hair out of her face. "But I like giving you what you need more. And, this time, you needed to be in charge."

"Thank you, Cam. For everything." She snuggled closer, her lips brushing his neck in a sweet little kiss. "I don't know what I'd do without you."

And she was gone, carried away from him by exhaustion and the release of orgasm. Pressing a kiss to her forehead, he pulled the blanket up over them both and held her through the rest of the night.

Chapter Nineteen

"*Chica*, you read this yet?" Miguel wheeled his chair across the aisle and slapped a stapled stack of papers on her desk.

"What is it?" Eva picked them up and scanned the first page—the autopsy report on Soup. "Good. I've been wondering when we'd get this."

"You won't be sayin' 'good' once you read it."

She lowered the papers. "Uh-oh. Don't tell me the case just got complicated."

"Case got complicated," he said with a grave nod.

"Damn. All right, give me the Cliff's Notes version."

"Soup had enough heroin in his system to kill five healthy men. Medical examiner says his heart would have stopped before he was able to finish injecting himself with this high of a dose. There was also some postmortem bruising on his arms, suggesting he was held down. Lots of bruising at the injection site, too."

"So," Eva said and the glow left over from the last three nights she'd spent with Cam faded. "Someone did it for him."

"And not at our crime scene. Lividity proves Soup was moved several hours after time of death, which the M.E. puts sometime late in the evening two Fridays ago."

Meaning Cam was probably the last person to see Soup alive. Which would not look good in a report.

Shit.

"You gonna call Wilde?" Miguel asked, reading her mind.

"He's not involved in Soup's murder." That much she knew with a hundred percent certainty—but he *was* holding something back from her. He had been since she first interviewed him, but she kept brushing it off as nothing.

Now, it was something.

Pain's jagged edge cut her to the core at the thought of Cam lying to her. She wanted to talk to him. Alone. Wanted to hear what he had to say, which was not standard operating procedure when interviewing a witness. "We should go see him."

Miguel lifted his brows. "*We*? You mean, in an official capacity?"

Her stomach twisted. "Absolutely. We're handling this the right way."

By the time Miguel stopped his department-owned car in front of the Wilde Security office, Eva had worked up a good, frothing anger. Why would Cam not tell her everything he knew? He wasn't involved in the murder, so what did he have to hide? And why the fuck would he hide it from her, of all people?

She banged through the front door, the little bell on the jamb shuttering in complaint, and spotted just the person she wanted to unleash her anger on sitting at one of the three desks, working on a computer. "Cam—"

"Vaughn," he corrected without looking up and hooked a thumb over his shoulder. "Cam's in with Greer."

She growled and stormed by him. "Dammit, grow your hair out again."

"Working on it." Vaughn stopped typing and stood, his hands flattened on his desk. He glanced between her and Miguel. "What's going on?"

Ignoring him, she strode to the back of the room and shoved into Greer's office. As the door slammed against the wall, Cam stopped talking with his oldest brother and did a double-take, slowly rising to his feet.

"Hey. Is everything okay?"

"No." She pointed at him, indicating he should stay seated, and then nodded to Miguel to shut the door behind them. Except Vaughn stood between the jambs, arms crossed over his chest, and Miguel didn't even attempt it.

Greer scowled. "What the hell is going on?"

"A murder investigation. You don't like it, you can get the fuck out of my way. In fact, you should. I don't need to talk to you." She rounded on Cam, fury burning like acid in her throat. He watched her with calm, unreadable eyes, which only served to tick her off more. She hated—*hated*— that he was sitting there so calmly, all the while withholding information from her.

"What's this about?" he asked, directing the question to Miguel.

She pinned her partner with a glare, daring him to answer. Miguel held up his hands and backed up a step. Damn right. This interview was hers. If anyone deserved answers from Cam, it was the woman he'd been fucking just about every night for the past week.

She jabbed her thumb toward her sternum. "Me, Cam. You're talking to me."

"All right." Still completely unruffled, he turned in his seat to face her. "You want to start by telling me why you're so pissed off at me? 'Cause, I gotta be honest, I'm lost."

"Soup was murdered. Not an overdose. *Murder.*"

Cam shut his eyes, breathed out a slow breath. When he met her gaze again, there was no shock. He *knew*. All along, he'd known Soup had been murdered, or at very least, he'd suspected it. And he hadn't said one word to her about it. Fury and hurt warred for space in her chest. Fury won. "Why the fuck didn't you tell me?"

"It's my mess." His voice was low with no hint of apology. "I'll clean it up."

"Hang on," Greer said and stared at his brother. "Is this the same informant that told you about the contract on your head?"

Eva's breath caught in her lungs. "*What?*"

From the doorway behind her, Vaughn cursed. "Cam, you didn't tell her? Goddammit, that is so like you." He moved into the room, putting himself between her and Cam. "Soup said someone tried to hire him for a hit, but Cam keeps brushing it off as no big deal."

"It *is* no big deal," Cam said. "I'm looking into it, and so far, I've found little evidence—"

"But you have found something," Greer stated.

"The only thing I know for sure is that Soup had five-hundred dollars after someone offered him a thousand to kill me."

Horror twisted Eva's stomach, adding to the nauseating slurry of emotion inside her. "You lied to me."

Wincing, Cam shouldered past his twin and tried to touch her, but she jerked away. He dropped his hand to his side. "It wasn't exactly a lie. More like an omission."

"Lying by omission is still lying!" All of the anger mutated into something much uglier. Something like betrayal. Oh, and hurt. Definitely a good dose of that swirling through her blood. "Cam, you lied to me during an official interview. That's obstruction. I can arrest you for that. I *should* arrest you for that."

"Whoa, hold up," Cam said, and his own temper sparked in his eyes. "I didn't lie during the interview. You asked me what I had met Soup about that night, I told you it was in regards to a case we were working. That was the truth. I just didn't go in to specifics about *which* case. You asked me where Soup got my jacket, I told you I gave it to him. You asked me about the money he had, I told you I didn't know where it came from."

"But you did. If someone paid him—"

"No, I didn't know that at the time. I suspected a lot of things, but until you came in here and told me definitively that Soup was murdered, I had no proof to substantiate any of my suspicions."

"Bullshit." Her voice wobbled and she hated herself for it. She threw back her shoulders, lifted her chin, and nailed him with a glare. "You *lied* to me." And the pain of his betrayal cut so deep into her chest, she didn't know if she'd ever breathe normally again.

Cam rubbed his face with both hands. "All right, yes." His arms dropped back to his sides in a gesture of defeat. "I lied. To you, to my brothers. I didn't want any of you involved. I can't risk anyone else getting hurt just because some asshole thinks I'd look better in a casket."

"It's my *job* to be involved. And I can handle myself, fuck you very much." She shoved him hard enough that he staggered. "You, of all people, should know that."

"I know you can," he said, straightening himself. "Believe me, I know. But no matter how well you're trained, horrible things can happen. Look at Seth Harlan. And my Dad? He was career military, and he and Mom still wound up bleeding to death in a gas station parking lot because someone wanted their car."

He stepped forward and wrapped his arms around her. Abruptly, she realized everyone else had vacated the room.

"I can't risk losing you, Eva. I just…can't."

Christ, she'd fucked this up. She was supposed to come in as a law enforcement officer and get an official statement. Instead, she'd let her emotions get the best of her and now here she stood, clinging to Cam like he'd vanish if she let him go.

And it took a helluva lot more willpower to yank out of his embrace than it should have. "News flash, Cam. You can't lose what you don't have."

His eyes, now more gray than blue, sparked with a flare of temper. "Nobody can take care of Eva like Eva, that it?"

"Damn right. I'm not yours to protect."

He laughed, but it was a nasty, sardonic sound that raked over her nerve endings. "Because God forbid you ever let anyone close enough to care for you."

She stared at him, her breath sawing in and out of her lungs with the force of her fury. "Don't you fucking dare turn this around on me. You're the one lying about everything and you're the one in danger. Not me. Not your brothers. So get your head outta your ass, Camden."

A muscle jumped in his jaw, but he didn't move, didn't say anything more, and for a half second, she felt like a complete bitch for throwing his fears in his face.

But, no. Dammit, she wasn't going to feel guilty for pointing out the obvious.

Unable to stand the deepening silence between them, she backed to the door. "You need to make an official statement. Again. We're going to have to investigate Soup's claims."

"It's a dead end," he said, jaw still clenched.

"That will be for us to decide. Miguel will take your statement." Blindly, she reached out for the door, found the handle, and all but fell through. Miguel waited on the other side, his expression grim. She hooked a thumb over her shoulder. "Can you find out what's going on?"

"Sure. Are you okay?"

Not in the least. Cam lied to her. The only person in her life she could count on to always tell the truth, and he'd lied.

"Yeah," she answered, telling a whooper of a lie herself. "I'm just…taking a personal day."

He nodded and patted her shoulder. "Good idea, *chica*. It's long overdue."

Chapter Twenty

In the short distance to the door, Eva got three offers for a ride back to the police station from Greer, Reece, and Vaughn, and declined them all. She didn't want to be around any of Cam's brothers, and especially didn't want to be cooped up in a car with them for any length of time, so she walked a couple blocks until she found a taxi. Her phone started buzzing, vibrating against her hip, the moment she slid into the cab's backseat and told the driver her destination.

What now?

She snapped it up and checked the screen. Preston. Right. She definitely was not in the mood to talk to him...

But instead of hitting ignore, her thumb hovered over the answer button.

A little voice told her she'd regret it. That she was only considering answering his call out of hurt pride and spite.

Fuck it.

She hit answer and pressed the phone to her ear. "Hello."

Preston's shock carried over the line in his voice. "Eva! You answered. I mean—how are you?"

Yup, she already regretted it. "What do you want, Preston?"

"Have you given any thought to what we talked about last week?"

"No," she admitted. "And I don't think—"

"Please," he interrupted, a tinge of desperation in his voice. "Just one date. Dinner. That's all I ask."

Eva stared out the window at the piles of gray snow lining the road. Cam lied. Preston cheated. What made one any different from the other? They both hurt about the same.

"Eva, are you still there?"

She heaved out a sigh. "Okay. One date."

Cam dropped into a chair after Miguel left with his statement, pressed his fingers into his eyelids to push back his thundering headache, and cursed himself out in every way he could think of—and a few he made up. He still stood behind his reasoning for not telling Eva about his suspicions, except maybe he could have gone about the whole thing differently. No idea how, but there must have been a way to keep her out of it without hurting her. He knew she saw him as her rock, something stable to cling to when her life got too hectic and his lie had ruptured that foundation. And, dammit, he knew how she felt about lies. How many times had she told him over the years that she loved his honesty? How much she loved that, no matter what, she could always count on him to tell her the truth?

And the most fucked up thing about that? He'd done nothing but lie to her since day one. Friendship? Hell, he'd never wanted that from her. He loved her and had kept his lips sealed, never once opening up and telling her the truth about his feelings.

Like she'd said, lying by omission was still lying.

She was *never* going to forgive him.

He felt three huge bodies crowd around him and groaned without opening his eyes. His brothers saw him the same way as Eva had. He was always the steady one, the reliable one. And, honestly, he was fucking sick of being everyone's support system. What did *he* have to hold onto?

"So…" Reece said, drawing the word out.

Greer wasn't as patient. "Wanna explain to us what the fuck you were thinking, Camden? You told me this wasn't a big deal, and I believed you."

Vaughn smacked him upside the head. "*That* was for lying to us." Another smack. "And that's for lying to Eva."

Cam shot to his feet and pushed through the barricade his brothers made before his twin decided to smack him again. "I fucked up, all right?"

"I'll say." Reece, the outwardly calmest of the three, crossed his arms in front of him and perched on the edge of Greer's desk. A stack of papers fell to the floor. He raised an eyebrow at the mess and then spared his oldest brother a disgusted glance. "We need to hire you a secretary." Then he returned his attention to Cam. "And we need to figure out this problem of yours before anyone else ends up dead."

"I have it handled, guys."

"You're not handling it alone," Greer said through his

teeth. "I already told you, that's not how this family works."

"Yeah, and you're not Dad." As soon as the words left Cam's mouth, he wanted to take them back. After their parents died, Greer had filed for emancipation, worked his ass off to finish school early, and got a fulltime job, then did his best to cobble together a semblance of the family they had lost. On his seventeenth birthday, he'd joined the military solely so he could better support them. He'd taken on more responsibility than any teenager should ever have to and it wasn't fair of Cam to condemn him for it now.

Greer remained as stoic as ever, but the words must have been like a physical blow. Cam opened his mouth to apologize, but what could he really say? The damage had been done and *I'm sorry* wasn't going to fix it.

"Tell us everything you know about Soup's death," Greer said after a long moment. "Do you have any suspects?"

He nodded. Soup and the hit contract were so much easier than the minefield he'd stepped into with his heartless remark. "I went through some of my old cases, focusing on the recent parolees that had threatened me in the past, and came up with three names—Arnold Mabry, Tom Lindquist, Gordon Dunphy. I've already eliminated Mabry. He didn't even remember me, and I never considered him a real suspect anyway. His was a crime of passion, and he was drunk when he made those threats against me."

"And the other two?" Reece asked.

"I haven't had any luck finding Lindquist. He's skipped out on his parole officer and there's a warrant for his arrest."

Everyone looked at Vaughn in silent question.

"Yeah," Vaughn said, "I'm on Lindquist."

Cam's stomach twisted and he faced his twin. "You

should sit this one out, bro. It's too—"

"If you say 'dangerous,' I am going to hit you again. And this time, it won't be a love tap."

Fuck, he hated this. If something happened to Vaughn or any of his brothers because of this case...

Unable to stay still, he paced across the office. "I need some air."

Greer stepped in front of the door, blocking his exit. "We're not done. Tell us about Dunphy."

"There's nothing to tell. I haven't looked into him yet. I had a restraining order against him for a while after he attacked me in a bar, but it's not active anymore. And, honestly, he doesn't have any reason to come after me now. I have no influence over his brother's case."

Greer nodded once. "I'll take a look at him. Reece, dig into Cam's old cases and see if you can't find us more suspects. We're gonna turn over every rock and see what comes scampering out."

The air hit Cam like an icy hammer to the face when he stepped outside, and he gratefully sucked it down until his lungs burned from the cold. Something damn near panic had sunk its claws into his heart, and he hadn't been able to draw a full breath inside the office.

He had to fix this. Throw himself into the investigation and figure out who was behind the contract before his brothers had time to get in too deep. Whoever it was hadn't had a problem killing Soup, so that person would also have no qualms about offing a handful of private investigators for asking the wrong questions in the wrong places.

He couldn't let that happen.

But first, he had to find Eva. Explain himself. Beg forgiveness. Then ask her not to pursue Soup's information because the thought of her getting caught in the crossfire just about crippled him.

And it was time to come clean about more than this case. All these years, he'd kept his relationships few and far between—just enough to take the edge off because his heart had never been into any of those women. His heart belonged to Eva and, fuck it, he wanted her too badly not to give this thing between them a shot. So he couldn't give her exactly what she wanted. Maybe his love would be enough. At least, he hoped it'd be enough. And if it wasn't—well, maybe he could try to do things her way. Marriage, two-point-five kids, a dog, a minivan, and a motherfucking white picket fence. Either way, he couldn't let his personal demons paralyze him into inaction anymore.

If he did, he got the sickening feeling he'd lose her forever.

The restaurant wasn't anything Eva would have picked for dinner, casual but with a faint enough whiff of upscale that she wasn't one-hundred percent comfortable. Preston was all smiles as he pulled out her chair for her and settled across the table. He'd ordered them red wine, which she hated. She took a sip anyway because she thought a splash of alcohol would do her good.

Then again, alcohol is what got her into this mess in the

first place.

She nudged the wine glass away precisely because the temptation to get drunk was so great. Like mother, like daughter.

"I'm so glad you agreed to meet me," Preston said, shaking out his napkin.

God, this was a mistake. She pushed away from the table. "I shouldn't have."

"No. Eva, wait." He scrambled around the table and caught her hand. "Please, hear me out. Garth Brooks will come on the radio, and I'll remember that town in West Virginia, the one we got stranded in when my car overheated? Remember you played darts at the dive bar with all those bikers? You impressed the heck out of me that night."

She smiled, relaxing a little at the memory. It had been a fun trip, one of the best she'd ever taken with him. "They loved us until they found out I'm a cop."

He released a breath as if relieved that she remembered. "And I can't even watch a Nationals game anymore because you're not sitting beside me making inappropriate comments about the opposing team. I miss us. I miss what we had."

She pulled her hand from his grasp. "How can you say that? You cheated on me. After I specifically told you when we first started dating that cheating is a stupid, high-schooler thing to do, and if you ever found someone you'd rather be with than me, you should just tell me."

"Yes," he admitted.

"But instead of telling me you wanted someone else—"

"I don't. Will you let me explain?"

She refused to answer. She didn't want an explanation. She wanted to get the hell out of here.

Taking her silence as a go ahead, he continued, "There's this permeating idea that a man can't get anywhere in the modern political climate without the right kind of wife backing him and—this is no excuse, but you don't fit that mold. Lark does, and I'm ashamed to say, I gave in to the pressure. I made a horrible mistake, Eva. I hope you can forgive me, and maybe, if I haven't screwed things up too badly, you can give us another chance?" He dropped to one knee in front of her, and her heart dropped right along with him.

Oh no. What the fuck did he think he was doing?

She grabbed his arms, urging him to stand. "Preston, no. Don't."

Ignoring her, he produced a little black box and opened it. A large marquise diamond sparked in the soft restaurant lighting, faintly blue against the white satin lining. "Please."

At her back, an excited murmur rippled through the other diners, and heat rose into her face. For a solid minute, she couldn't come up with a thing to say in response. "Preston—"

"You don't have to answer now," he added in a rush. He stood and closed the box, pressing it into her hand. "I know this is a lot to take in. I had planned to wait, but I have to let you know how serious I am this time."

Panic skated down the back of her neck. "What about Lark?"

"I broke it off with her right after we got back from Key West. I regret hurting her, but she's the woman everyone thought I should marry, not the one I wanted, and I'm done listening to everyone. I want *you*, nobody else."

Not that long ago, it would have been so easy to say yes, to throw herself into his arms and sink back into the comfort of a relationship with him. Now there were too many variables. Would she ever be able to completely trust him again? And what about Cam? Going back to Preston would mean the end of their friends with benefits relationship. Would they be able to go back to a plain old friendship? Or, oh God, would she lose him completely?

Pain bloomed in the center of her chest at the thought of losing Cam, and yet she could not tell Preston no. She tried. The word was on her tongue, but wouldn't leave her lips.

Two years. She'd spent two years of her life with this man. Five if she counted the years he'd spent pursuing her before they officially started dating. That had to mean something. At the very least, he deserved more consideration from her than a flat-out rejection.

Everyone made mistakes, right?

Even Cam was not immune to them. He'd proved that today by lying to her.

"I'll think about it," she said.

Preston pulled her into his arms, and a round of scattered applause came from the other restaurant patrons. No doubt, they all thought she said yes. She stared down at the box in her hand.

Maybe she should have.

Chapter Twenty-One

"I figured I'd find you here."

Eva flinched at the sound of Cam's voice. She'd come to Maguire's because work was out of the question after making a fool out of herself in front of Miguel this afternoon, and home didn't seem like a good idea either. Maguire's dark interior, smelling of beer, fried food, and decades of cigarette smoke, was comforting, a security blanket masquerading as a cop bar. But she should have guessed Cam would come looking for her here.

He settled at the bar beside her and flagged the bartender, who acknowledged him with a smile and short wave before pouring a pint of Guinness and bringing it over. He waited until the bartender left to tend other patrons before spinning on his stool and facing her.

"Listen, I'm sorry. I shouldn't have lied, and you have every reason to hate me."

She heaved out a sigh. "I don't hate you, Cam." She

didn't think it would be possible to hate the man.

"You have every right to be pissed as hell," he said.

"And I am. Absolutely. But," she added, even though she didn't want to make the admission, "I know you and I get your reasoning." She aimed a scowl at him. "It still really fucking hurts you lied to me. I thought you were the one person I could trust without a doubt and then you went and pulled this shit."

He spread his hands in a gesture of supplication. "I'm an idiot."

"I've been hearing that a lot lately."

Out of the corner of her eye, she saw his brows draw together. Then he noticed the ring box sitting on the bar in front of her. He nudged it. "What's that?"

"A ring."

Setting down his beer, he scooped up the box and opened it before she could stop him. His jaw tightened. "Preston gave you this?"

"Earlier tonight," she said as a flush worked into her cheeks. She didn't know what she had to be ashamed about, but there it was. "I went to dinner with him."

The blue of Cam's eyes darkened to a turbulent gray. "Why?"

"Why not?"

He growled at her non-answer. "Are you seriously accepting this?"

"I don't know."

"You don't know? How can you even consider it after what he did to you?"

Wincing because he had a point, she struggled to find the words to make him understand. "We were together for years, Cam. It's hard to throw that much time away."

"And what about *our* years together?"

She hesitated. "That's different."

"Why? Because we weren't sleeping together?"

"Yes."

"Well, we are now," he said and snapped the ring box closed. "So what about us? You're just going to throw us away?"

Stunned, she gaped at him. "There is no *us*. Not like that, at least. The sex, as amazing as it is between us, was always meant to be just sex, remember? You're the one that said it's not a permanent situation."

He held up the ring box. "But this is?"

"Maybe…?" Groaning, she dropped her head into her arms.

"Does Preston make you happy?" His voice sounded strained, and she lifted her head. Pain—real, stark pain—etched itself into his expression.

"Oh, fuck. I don't know," she confessed. "I need you to be my best friend right now, okay? You always give me the best advice."

"Yeah, well, you want some friendly advice?" He flipped up the top of the box again and shoved it across the bar until it was right under her nose. "If a man really loves you, he'd never buy *this* ring. He'd know it's too big for your taste. He'd know that you'll never wear it because it'll rip right through latex gloves and get caught on everything at work. He'd know you're not a diamond kind of woman. He'd know your favorite color is red and get you a simple band of white-gold studded with rubies." He slapped a hand down in front of her and something metal clinked against the bar. He didn't lift his hand right away, but he didn't have to. She had a good idea what was under there.

Without another word, Cam grabbed his coat from the back of his seat, stuffed his arms in, and walked away. She watched him go, then stared down at the ring he'd left on the bar next to Preston's. It was just as he described, a thin white-gold band set with little princess-cut rubies.

Sick to her stomach, she picked up the two rings. Oh, no. He wasn't going to drop this goddamn grenade in front of her and walk away. She shoved away from the bar and ran out onto the street, the cold air stinging her eyes and lungs. She spotted Cam getting into his 4Runner, parked at the curb several cars down.

"Wilde." She chased after him and planted herself in front of the SUV, hands on her hips as she squinted at the headlights. The engine revved twice, but she stood her ground. "Vehicular homicide gets you three to fifteen years, buddy."

He shut off the headlights, leaving her seeing spots. With the engine still rumbling softly, he stood on the runner to glare at her over the top of the door.

"Cardoso," he said in the same frustrated tone she'd used. "Get outta the way."

She held up the ring. "What the hell is this?"

"Exactly what it looks like."

His grim expression took the air out of her lungs like a punch to the sternum. "Cam—" At a loss, she stared at him and struggled to find her voice. "But—but you can't seriously want to marry me. You're not the marrying type."

"No, I'm not, which should tell you everything you need to know about how fucking serious I am."

"That's ridiculous."

"Ridiculous?" He jumped down from the SUV and shut the door with a *bang* that echoed between the buildings lining the street. As snowflakes swirled in the air, he stalked toward her. This wasn't the easygoing, roll-with-the-punches Cam she was used to. Honestly, the intensity in him right now kind of frightened her, and part of her wanted to run—but, no, she'd done enough running from him.

She braced her shoulders, lifted her chin, and met his predatory gaze with a glare. "Yes. Ridiculous. How long have you had this thing?"

"About two hours." His arm snaked around her waist and dragged her toward his body. Hot, cinnamon scented breath fanned her cheek as he traced the line of her jaw with his lips.

Her hands flattened against his chest. She should push him away. She absolutely should, but the heat coming off him made her that much more aware of the cold air at her back, and she wanted to burrow into him, luxuriate in his warmth, breathe in the cinnamon and dark spice scent that always shot straight to her libido and was unique to Camden Wilde. His hard lips followed the curve of her ear, brushed over her closed eyes, down her nose. She shuddered, her fingers curling into the front of his coat of their own volition.

He hesitated over her mouth, their breaths mingling into a single cloud. His gaze lifted from its hungry perusal of her lips and met hers. She expected lust, heat, hunger. Instead, his blue eyes were resigned. Maybe even a little sad.

Groaning, he rested his forehead against hers. "I kept thinking if I was patient long enough, you'd see us for what we are."

Eva pushed against his chest and he released her without protest. Stepping back, she hugged herself to fend off the cold that suddenly pierced her to her core. "What do you think we are?"

"We're soul mates. The real deal."

Silence stretched between them as he waited for her to respond. But she couldn't come up with anything coherent. Cam, her soul mate? Not possible…

Was it?

Cam reached out to tuck a stray strand of hair behind her ear. "The last five years have been a lie. Well, an *omission*. I'm good at those."

Confusion and horror battled it out inside her chest, neither one gaining ground over the other, and her mind outright refused to comprehend the words coming out of his mouth. She massaged the headache in her temple with a shaking hand. "I don't understand. Everything we've done together…?"

"No, that's not it. I've meant absolutely everything that's happened between us since day one, but I've always wanted more, and I never told you. I want you, Eva. I've always wanted you, but I'm done being patient. I'm not your partner. I'm not your fuck buddy. I'm not even your friend."

She sucked in a stunned breath as horror finally won out and dug icy claws into her heart. "What are you saying?"

"I can't continue to separate the friend you want me to be from the man who is crazy in love with you." He squeezed his eyes shut for a long moment, then shook his head and turned away. "So maybe it's time you find a new best friend."

Vaughn settled onto the stool beside her barely twenty minutes after Cam left her standing on the street with her head reeling. She wasn't at all surprised to see him. As soon as Cam showed up at home, Vaughn would have felt the need to go all protective "big" brother. Maybe that's why she'd hung around here. Waiting for him to come flay her alive.

Not that she didn't already feel like an open, throbbing wound.

"You know," Vaughn said conversationally, plucking a red straw from the napkin holder on the bar and sticking it between his teeth. "I can make you disappear and nobody will ever find your body."

She slid him an incredulous sideways glance. Amazing he could look so much like Cam, and yet…not. He always carried himself like he was spoiling for a fight, and the flat-ness in his blue eyes warned *back off or get hurt*. He was one scary dude. Not someone she'd want to cross paths with while unarmed on a dark street, especially after the sunny statement he just made.

"You know," she replied in the same conversational tone, "that's called premeditated murder and carries a twenty-five-to-life sentence."

He lifted one shoulder, then smiled as the busty bar-tender set a short glass of rum and Coke in front of him. Either he'd ordered before he sat down or he was as much a regular at Maguire's as she was. She bet on the former. A cop shop like Maguire's wasn't his usual scene.

"I'm not saying I will," he said after a long, appreciative drink. "But I can. Actually, I should because you've done nothing but make my brother miserable since Key West. If I remember correctly, we had a talk about the consequences for that."

"You mean when you threatened me at the reception."

"Ah-ah." He wagged a finger. "I don't make threats."

"And what exactly do you call this?"

"I'm giving you an ultimatum."

She stared. "Ultimatum?" Indignation made her slam her bottle down on the bar with more force than necessary. "What? Stop fucking Cam or else?"

"I don't care if you fuck him twice a day and three times on Sunday. Good for him if you do." He tapped his temple. "It's the mind fucking I don't like. You need to make a decision. It's either Cam or that asshole you're so hung up on. But if you choose Preston, you need to let Cam go. Cut all ties."

Cut all ties with Cam? Her stomach pitched at the thought. "That's not fair, Vaughn. You can't ask me to — "

He faced her, and she gulped back the rest of her protest. His eyes were no longer flat and expressionless, but had ignited into cold fury. "No, I'll tell you what's not fair. Cam's always right there when you need him, even if that means leaving his own brother's wedding. You tell him to jump, and he'll reach for the moon. He's put his whole goddamn life on hold for you. What have you done for him besides give him a few good lays?"

Eva opened her mouth, but found she had no breath to respond. Vaughn finished his drink in a gulp and dug some cash out of the pocket of his jeans. He stood and peeled off a few bills for the bartender's tip.

"Vaughn." She grasped his arm. "I'm sorry."

His lips tightened into a thin line, but he didn't glance down at her as he extracted himself from her grip. "I'm not the one you should be saying that to."

Chapter Twenty-Two

Eva left Maguire's with the sense that her entire world had just imploded, and it only got worse when she drove home to find Preston's car waiting in her driveway. He shut off the engine and got out when she parked beside him.

Exasperated, she shoved open her door and climbed out, meeting him at the gate to her yard. "You have to stop doing this."

His smile of greeting faded into a scowl. "I can't stop by my girlfriend's house?"

Christ, how could a smart man be so fucking clueless? "Okay, one: I'm not your girlfriend." She held up a finger, ticking the points off as she made them. "And two: I saw you less than four hours ago. What gives? You never used to be this clingy."

He sputtered. "I'm not clingy."

"Four hours ago, Preston. And, no, I haven't decided to take you back, so if that's why you're here—"

"No. No, that's not—I just—I missed you." He leaned in, and she could have avoided it, but the beginnings of an epiphany niggled at the back of her mind, and she had to know if it was right. His lips touched hers, soft and cool—and she felt nothing. Not the slightest stirring of desire. She wanted hot and hard. A command, not a request. As Preston's hand slid down her arm, everything in her revolted.

He was not Camden Wilde.

She broke away from him and reached for the gate before he had a chance to recover. By the time he scrambled through, she'd already crossed the yard and was halfway up her porch steps.

"Eva, wait." He caught her hand and tugged her to a stop. "What's wrong?"

She shrugged out of his grasp. "We're not right for each other anymore, Preston. If we ever were. You must see that. I'm not your type."

Something dark flashed through his eyes. "You don't know crap about my type."

"Maybe not," she admitted, found his ring box in her pocket, and handed it to him. "But I know you're not mine. I'm sorry. My answer is no. It's just not going to work out between us."

His hand closed around her arm again, and he jerked her around when she tried to continue up the steps. "Is it someone else?"

"Let go of me."

For a startling second, she didn't think he would. And in that second, she caught a glimpse of violence, the kind she'd seen in the eyes of murderers who felt no regret for their crimes. She yanked against him, and he released her, then backed off.

"Camden," he said. Not a question, but a disgusted statement.

She didn't bother confirming or denying. Frankly, it was none of his business whom she chose, because it was not him.

His face flushed a deep red, and his hands curled into fists at his sides. In all the years she'd known him, she'd never seen him angry—and now he looked like he was going to blow his top. A trickle of fear sent her heart rate up a few beats per minute and she took a step backwards before she caught herself.

"Do what you want with it," he said, throwing the ring box back at her, then stomped to his car. Tires squealed on the wet pavement, and he leaned on the horn as he peeled out.

Shelby came to the front door with a package of Twizzlers in hand and peered through the screen. "What the fuck was all that noise?"

"A childish tantrum." Man, she wished she'd seen him get angry years ago. You could tell a lot about a person from the way they handled anger, and what she saw in Preston just now made her wince in embarrassment for him.

Shelby stared after his car. "Preston threw a tantrum?"

"Like a three year old."

Shelby snorted before ducking back inside. "And you say *I* have bad taste in men."

Poe squawked a greeting from his perch in the living room. Eva walked to him and ruffled the feathers on top of his head with one finger. "You have *horrible* taste in men, Shel—except for this guy."

Shelby waved a piece of licorice at her. "Need I remind you, none of my past boyfriends have ever thrown a temper tantrum on our front lawn?"

"Because Poe has a higher IQ than any of your past boyfriends. You might as well have been dating vegetables."

"Ooo, good one." With a grin, Shelby bit into her candy and sketched a point in the air. "Big sis, one. Shelby, zero. And, sadly, you're right. But only because I have the smartest birdie in the world."

"Can't argue that."

They both cooed over the bird for a moment. Poe flapped his wings and puffed out his chest, soaking in every bit of the attention.

"So," Shelby said as they settled on the couch together. An Asian horror movie played on the TV, and Shel used the remote to pause it. "Preston's out of the picture?"

"After that? Yeah." Eva sighed and stole a piece of licorice. "Way out."

"Good. BRB." She bounced up from the couch and vanished down the hallway.

"Did you really just say BRB?" Eva called after her. "You're spending way too much time online. Maybe it's time you find a job."

"I have one."

Eva stared as her sister reemerged from the hallway with her hands behind her back. "You do? Where?"

"The coffee shop where I met Cam's brother. The one I've been going to for breakfast? I like it there, so I applied for a barista position. They called today." She lifted her shoulders. "It's no big deal."

Oh, yes it was. Shelby had never before taken the

initiative and done something responsible like find herself a job. Maybe there was hope for her yet.

Eva wanted to hug her—oh, what the hell. She moved around the coffee table and pulled her sister into her arms. "Good for you, Shel. I'm really happy for you."

"Didn't believe me when I told you I'm turning my life around?"

"No. But can you blame me? We've both heard that line so many times from Mom, and it never happened."

"Mom's not well. We both know it." Grief strained Shelby's usually bright smile. The purples around her eye had faded in the week since their mother's visit, leaving the bruise several ugly shades of yellow. "And I don't want to end up like her any more than you do. We're not so different, Evie. We're just taking alternate routes to the same place.

"And, okay," she admitted before Eva could form a re-ply, "I went a little too far trying to prove how I'm not Mom, only to realize I was turning in to a punk rock version of her." She stepped back and pressed a picture frame into Eva's palm. "But you? Evie, you haven't gone far enough. You've played it safe, dating wimpy, passive-aggressive men like Preston, the exact opposite of the asshole boyfriends Mom brought home."

"I know."

"And then there's Cam."

"No, we're not talking about him."

"Yeah, we are. Think about it. Who did you call as soon as we had Mom under control the other night?"

Dammit, did she have to acknowledge it?

Shelby nudged her when she stayed silent too long and she muttered, "Cam."

"And that's not the first time you turned to him. Who do you call whenever you're sick or sad or lonely?"

"Of course I call Cam. He is—*was* my best friend. Now, I don't know." And that killed her. She missed what they used to be, but at the same time, she didn't want to go back to plain old friendship. She'd gotten too comfortable with Cam as a lover. "Dammit. Having sex with him was such a huge mistake."

"Oh, God." Shelby rolled her eyes, the gesture highlighting her fading bruises. "You're such a dunce sometimes. He's not your best friend. Honestly, he never was. He's the guy who's wild for you, who would do anything for you. He's *nothing* like Mom's boyfriends, yet you pushed him to the back burner. And still, he stuck. He's always going to stick and everyone with two eyes—hell," she gestured to her bruises, "with *one* eye—can see how much he loves you. So why can't you see it?"

Eva moistened her suddenly dry lips and looked down at the framed photo from her dresser that showed her and Cam after a Tough Mudder event, arms looped around each other. They were both soaked head-to-toe in mud and grinning at each other.

"Look at it," Shelby told her.

"I've seen it before." She'd had this photo for three years, had seen it every morning as she readied for work.

"But you've never really looked at it. Look at his expression."

She did and saw exactly what Shelby wanted her to see, what Shelby had probably seen all along. Love. His eyes were soft and crinkled at the corners, and his smile was one of complete adoration. She thought of Cam's ring in her pocket, the vibrant red gems speaking of the out-of-control fire and passion they shared in the bedroom. And, if she was honest with herself, out.

"He scares me," she admitted, stroking a finger over his face in the photo.

"Why, because you can't control him?"

"Because I can't control myself around him."

Shelby gave a soft laugh and poked her in the ribs with one finger. "You ask me, Evie, that's a really awesome problem to have."

*H*e's *the guy who is wild for you, who would do anything for you.*

The truth of her sister's words bounced around in Eva's skull all night, until she finally gave up on sleeping and settled on the couch to watch TV with a box of old photos. In every single one, she saw the same thing as in the picture on her dresser: Cam loved her. And as the photos progressed, she started to see that adoration reflected in her own eyes and smile.

Oh, hell. Why had she never noticed it before?

Shelby joined her around 2:00 am, but said nothing more about Cam or Preston or any of it. She just snuggled in beside Eva like she had when they were kids and entertained them both with snarky commentary on the late-night infomercials. Her imitation of the 1-900 phone sex commercials was eerily spot-on.

Eva narrowed her eyes at her little sister. "Shelby, you didn't ever…"

"Some things are better left unknown, sis."

"You're shitting me."

Shelby shrugged. "You do what you gotta. And it's not as risqué as you think. Those women? They're mothers and sometimes grandmothers, sitting at home in their pajamas with the TV on mute tuned to a sappy Lifetime movie, and their dogs or cats—or in my case, bird—snuggled up next to them."

"While a pervert gets off to your voice on the end other of the line?"

"For the most part, they're not pervs. They're just lonely and…" She shrugged again, this time with less sass in the movement, and focused on the TV screen. "Well, I know a thing or two about being lonely."

"Aw, Shel." Eva wrapped an arm around her shoulders and squeezed. "I've been thinking. The house is gonna be very quiet when you move out."

Shelby sat up, eyes wide. "Really?"

"Yeah. So…maybe you'd want to stick around."

With a sound that could only be described as a *squee*, Shelby tackled her to the couch in a hug.

"Thank you! I'll pay rent this time," she promised. "As soon as I start at the coffee shop, I'll help with the bills and buy groceries. I'll make you proud of me."

Eva nodded, afraid that forming a verbal response would end in a sobbing fit—and unlike her mother, she did not cry prettily. It was all red eyes, blotchy face, and snot, and once she started with the waterworks, she found it hard to stop.

As gently as she could, she peeled Shelby's arms from her around her neck and then cleared her throat. "How about a movie?"

"Ooo, good idea. I recorded *Sharknado*. Sharks and tornadoes in a *SyFy* original movie…you can't go wrong."

"Yeah," Eva had to admit, "sounds pretty awesome."

"I know, right? Awesomely horrible. Which calls for hip-widening junk food. And wine. White for you, red for me. We might as well class it up." Full of boundless energy, even in the middle of the night, Shelby sprang up and disappeared into the kitchen.

"Let Poe out so he can bask in the B-horror movie glory with us," Eva called after her and, a moment later, Poe flew out to perch on the arm of the sofa. She smiled and scratched the bird's chest. "You have a pretty good mama, you know that, buddy?"

Poe squawked as if in agreement.

Eva succumbed to exhaustion half way through *Sharknado,* and her dreams swirled with images of Cam. They were both in the movie, covered from head-to-toe in mud, running from the horrendous CG animation, and he threw himself in front of an attacking shark while shielding her from the winds of a tornado.

Then in the twisted time warp of dreamland, they were at Maguire's, and he gracefully bowed to her superiority in the game of darts before trouncing her in a pool match.

At his condo, in his shower, his mouth set fire to her nerve endings as his body took hers to new heights of erotic pleasure.

And then, she again saw the stark betrayal in his eyes when she'd admitted she was actually considering Preston's proposal….

Eva jolted awake early in the afternoon to an empty house, and every cell in her being demanded she find him.

She'd apologize. Hell, she'd grovel if that's what it took. Because she'd come to a stunningly obvious realization somewhere between Shelby's come-to-Jesus talk and the shark tornadoes: she never would have chosen Preston over Cam.

Never.

Cam made her laugh. He took away her control. Made her body sing with exquisite pleasure. Tied her up into jealous knots. Made her trust him. Alternately relaxed her and riled her up with just the sound of his voice. Made her happy in a way that nothing else in her life ever had. And she loved him to distraction. It was terrifying—a free fall, and she had no control of the parachute—but it was past time she told him what he meant to her.

If it wasn't already too late.

She hurried through a shower, tossed on some clothes, and was in her car before she remembered his ring. Leaving the engine running, she ran back inside and found it where she'd left it the night before on her dresser. She slid it onto her finger and, yeah, it belonged right there.

What would he say when he saw it? Her pulse kicked with an odd mix of trepidation and anticipation. Well, she'd find out soon enough.

Eva drove to his condo first, but Vaughn's Hummer sat in the driveway, and the space beside it reserved for Cam's 4Runner was empty. She floored it past the condo without stopping—didn't want to see Vaughn before she found Cam—and continued on toward the Wilde Security office, which was the only other place he'd be if he wasn't out on a case.

And there was the 4Runner, parked in one of the spaces in front of the office. From the looks of things, he was the only one there right now. At least she didn't have to grovel in front of his brothers. She would if it came to it, but she'd much rather have this conversation in private.

Except, now that she was here, trepidation was kicking anticipation's ass. She stopped her car just inside the parking lot entrance to calm her nerves.

What if he rejected her? It was nothing less than she deserved.

Through the swirling snow, she saw him leave the office and jog to his SUV, head bowed against the wind. He opened the door, and she saw her chance to talk to him slipping away.

Now or never.

She hit the button for her window, and cold air spilled inside as she leaned out. "Cam, wait!"

He paused and turned toward her voice. Brow furrowing under the brim of his winter hat, he started toward her.

His car exploded into a fireball.

The shock of it blew out her windshield and knocked her back against the seat, her ears ringing, her lungs struggling to drag in a full breath. Her skin felt hot, raw, scratched up from the glass, and as she blearily focused on her hands, she realized she was bleeding.

Cam.

Oh, God.

She scrambled out of her car, bits of glass tinkling onto the icy pavement as she staggered and tried to find her bearings. A black and red blur bolted past her. Cam wasn't wearing black. So who…?

Her mind finally started firing on all cylinders again. The bomber was here and trying to escape.

Hell no.

She spun, reaching out blindly to snag his coat. She missed, but he slipped when he tried to dodge her, pinwheeled across the ice, and ended up flat on his face several feet away. She jumped on his back, but discovered it was unnecessary—he'd knocked himself out when he fell. If only all criminals were so helpful. She made short work cuffing him, then scanned the scene. The 4Runner blazed sky high and the flames had spread to the office. She didn't see Cam, and pain like she'd never felt before cleaved her in half.

Where was he?

There. She spotted him lying face-down in the snow ten feet from where he'd stood when the bomb went off.

Unmoving.

No.

She raced across the lot to him, slipping and sliding, scrambling to find and dial her phone with numb fingers, but gave up on calling 9-1-1 when she heard the wail of sirens.

Please, please let him be alive.

She didn't dare touch him to roll him over, so she flattened herself out on her stomach next to him. She reached for his hand, but thought better of it when she noticed the burns already blistering his skin.

"Cam?" She couldn't keep the break from her voice. Didn't even try. "Cam, you hang on. Help's coming, okay?"

His eyes opened to blurry slits, and he tried to push himself upright.

She lay a gentle hand on his back, wincing at the heat rolling off his body. "Hey, no. Stay still."

A slow blink cleared some of the haziness from his eyes, and his lips peeled back from his teeth in a grimace of pain. "What. The. Fuck?"

Letting go a shaky laugh, Eva sat up beside him and pressed her palms to her face, the heat on her cheeks warming her icy fingers. She probably looked like she had a bad sunburn, but it didn't matter.

Cam would be okay.

And if she'd just stop shaking, so would she.

Chapter Twenty-Three

"Eva?"

As she stepped off the elevator, the woman's surprised voice stopped her in her tracks. Lark Warren stood in the hallway outside the room Cam was supposed to be in, as small and pale as a china doll in her ivory colored coat with her streaky brown hair pulled back into a sloppy knot on top of her head. She wore no make-up and looked as if she hadn't slept in a few days.

"Lark. Uh, hi. What are you doing here?"

"I was just…" She wrapped her arms around her middle and her cheeks flushed a pink that could only be described as pretty. "Visiting a friend."

A friend? She couldn't mean Cam…could she? Were they the kind of friends that visited each other in the hospital? Were they more than—

No. Eva shut down the line of thought before jealousy consumed her. Cam was a one woman kind of man. He wasn't a cheater—which made her feel like the lowest kind of slime now that she thought about it. Going out with Preston for dinner had been so incredibly wrong. Sure, she and Cam had never agreed to more than a friends-with-benefits relationship. No commitment, no exclusivity. But, dammit, he *never* would have dated someone else as long as he was sleeping with her.

So she had no reason to be jealous of Lark. Had to be her exhaustion talking. Nearly twenty-four hours had passed since the bomb went off, and between the craziness at the scene, the arrest and interrogation of her suspect, and the ensuing paperwork, she was only standing right now by the sheer power of her will because she refused to go home before she saw Cam.

A lump swelled in her throat and she lifted her chin, indicating the door to his room. "How is he?"

"You know…?" Lark's deer-in-the-headlights expression might have been comical if Eva wasn't fighting back a rising sense of panic.

"Yeah, I was there. Is he all right?"

The corners of her mouth turned down into a ridiculously pretty frown, and a crease appeared between her eyebrows. "What do you mean?"

Okay, not the brightest bulb, was she? "I saw the bomb. I got the guy that did it."

"Oh." And back to the wide-eyed deer expression. "Oh. Uh, I need to go."

"What?"

"I…need to go now."

Eva had been a detective long enough to know when she wasn't going to get answers from someone. She stepped out of the way, almost as eager to end the conversation as Lark was. "Sure. See ya."

Lark took a few quick steps down the hallway, but came up short and drew a breath that moved her shoulders. Appearing calmer, she spun back. "I'm sorry for how I acted in Key West. I had no idea about your past with Preston. He never told me about you."

"It's fine."

"No. It's totally not. If I had known..." She shook her head. "But at least we both figured out the kind of man he was before we made any stupid mistakes, right?"

"Wait, what—"

"I have to go. You didn't see me here." Without waiting for a response, Lark bypassed the elevator and took the stairs, the heavy fire door slapping shut behind her.

Weird.

But not important. Eva filed the conversation away for later consideration and strode to Cam's room. Right now, he was her only concern.

The lights had been dimmed in deference to the sleeping figure on the bed and Eva slowed her step, careful not to make any noise. Machines measured his heart beat with a steady *beep beep beep,* and all kinds of IV lines ran from bags hanging over his head into his body. He looked so thin, as if he'd dropped ten pounds overnight. His color was only a few pallid shades above the white blanket covering him— except for the bruises that discolored half of his swollen face with deep purple splotches and the burns mottling both of his arms with an angry red stain.

Oh, God. She could have lost him for good.

As she leaned over the bed rail, he opened eyes glassy with the pain meds in his system. "Hi."

He was awake. And talking. She barely checked the urge to throw her arms around him. The only thing stopping her was the possibility of hurting him. "Hi. You're okay?"

"Yeah," he said, his voice so full of gravel he didn't sound like himself. "No biggie."

Relief like she'd never felt before coursed through her veins and left her knees shaking. "Don't pull that macho it's-only-a-flesh-wound shit with me. You were blown up."

He laughed softly, but the movement of his ribcage caused a spike in his heart rate.

"Hey, don't do that." Worried, she swept his sweat-damp hair from his face. "Are you hurting?"

He winced. "As you just got done pointing out, Detective, I was blown up. So make that a resounding yes."

"Right. Stupid question. Can I do anything to help?"

"No." He tried shifting around in the bed, muttering a curse under his breath when he didn't move far. "What are you doing here anyway?"

Ouch.

But, yes, she completely deserved that after the way their last conversation ended. "I, um, have something to show you."

He arched a brow. "Is it something that might get you arrested for indecent exposure?"

"No. Pervert." She held up her right hand, wiggling her ring finger. "I made my decision."

"Yeah?" He squinted at her finger, but gave no hint of

recognition. "Nice ring. Suits you."

Wait. What? He couldn't have forgotten about giving it to her. Or about what her wearing it meant...

"Dammit, Vaughn!" She popped up from the bed and glowered down at him. If he wasn't already injured, she'd shoot him on principle. "You jackass, I thought you were Cam. What are you doing here?"

"Vacationing," Vaughn said, deadpan. "I always vacation at the hospital. This place is renowned for their gourmet cafeteria slop. You should try it. De-lish."

"Delish?" she echoed. "Are you high?"

He groped around at his side, found the button that administered On Demand morphine, then pressed it. "As a kite. They make the best drug cocktails here, too."

She shook her head, trying to wrap her mind around this staggering turn of events. "If *you* were driving that car, then Cam is—"

"In serious need of a shower," Vaughn said and grinned— or tried to grin at someone over her shoulder, but it looked more like a grimace. She whirled to find Cam standing in the doorway, alive and whole, if not a little haggard. Two days' worth of beard covered his jaw and his hair hadn't seen a comb in as many days. At the moment, he looked more like Vaughn than Vaughn did, which was probably the point— they hadn't corrected anyone on Vaughn's identity so they must be intent on keeping the switch a secret for the time being.

Cam's bloodshot eyes widened at the sight of her, but he otherwise ignored her presence and skirted the foot of the bed to stand on the other side. Worry etched lines into his expression as he stared down at his twin.

"Hey, bro. How are you feeling?"

"Like I've been blown up."

Cam winced. "You're not funny."

"I wish I was trying to be."

"For future reference, I'm not cool with you playing the hero and taking bullets—or car bombs—for me."

"For future reference, I'm not either."

"Good. Glad we got that settled. "

Feeling like an intruder, Eva backed away, but Vaughn's eyes drifted toward her in a *hint-hint* kind of way, and Cam finally lifted his head to meet her gaze. "Thanks for helping him."

Man, his tone was downright arctic. She'd have to check herself for frostbite later. "When I saw it happen, I thought you were…" She couldn't give voice to those dark thoughts and cleared her throat. "He was driving your car."

"Had a flat," Vaughn muttered. "Took the 4Runner 'cause Cam was working from home under orders from Greer."

"And by that, you mean you slashed your own tire," Cam corrected, frustration and a heavy dose of fear making his voice rusty. "Then you took the 4Runner, stole my wallet, and purposely dangled yourself as bait."

Vaughn tilted his head in acknowledgement. "Had to be done." He looked at Eva and explained, "I found Tom Lindquist. He told me he'd been approached about the hit, but had refused it. He gave me the name of someone he thought wouldn't refuse and hinted that it was going down sooner rather than later. I had to do something."

Cam's hands tightened on the bed railing. "Fuck you, Vaughn. Putting yourself at risk like that? You could have died, and it would have killed me as good as a bullet."

"Ditto," Vaughn said, and underneath all the swelling, his eyes went steely. "You know how much it fucking scared me when I found out someone was going to try for you? I had to do something. You would have done the same."

The twins locked stares until Vaughn drew in a breath that caused him to wince. He looked over at her again, something close to a plea in his eyes. "Eva, tell him he's being an ass."

No way. Things were already bad enough between them.

She kept her gaze on Cam, and instead tried to express everything she felt with her eyes. "It scared the hell out of me when I thought he was you."

Cam nodded once, curtly, but said nothing more. Self-conscious in the face of his coolness, she stuffed her hands in her jeans pockets.

Vaughn gave a noisy sigh through his nose when she didn't speak again. "Oh, c'mon, Eva. At least tell him what you came in here to tell me when you thought I was him."

Cam lifted his eyebrows in question, but still said nothing.

Okay, so he was going to make her work for this. She didn't blame him. "Can we step out into the hall?"

He looked at his brother, worry written all over his face, as if he was afraid to leave the bedside. Vaughn gave an almost imperceptible nod, communicating with him in their non-verbal way, both of them probably saying a shitload of meaningful things without opening their mouths.

Cam finally straightened away from the bed and walked toward the door without another word. She followed and tried to formulate everything she wanted to say to him into a coherent list.

Number one: I'm sorry.

Number two: I'm an idiot for not seeing what was right in front of me this whole time.

Number three: You're *an idiot for not telling me how you felt years ago.*

Number four: Don't you ever fucking scare me like that again.

Number five—

She realized Cam was staring at her and sucked in a deep breath. But when she opened her mouth, all that came out was a faint, "How's Vaughn?"

"He has several broken ribs, a bruised lung, a ruptured spleen, and a broken leg. Burns, bruises all over. The docs are monitoring him for internal blood loss. He may need surgery." Listing his brother's injuries seemed to drain the last bit of energy out of him and his shoulders sagged. He propped his back against the wall and crossed his arms in front of him. She wished she dared reach out and pull him into her arms, but would he accept her comfort or push her away? The part of her that feared he would push her away kept her rooted to the spot in the middle of the hallway, and she rocked back and forth on her feet, hands still in her pockets.

"But he'll be okay?"

"It could have been worse. He'll be healing for a long time, but he will heal."

"Good. That's…good." She mentally flailed for something more to say. "Uh, it was Gordon Dunphy. I caught him trying to escape. He says he was paid to do it, but won't give up the person who hired him until he has a plea deal on the table."

"I know," Cam said, his jaw tightening.

Desperate to delay the conversation they really needed to have for a few moments longer, she continued, "Charles Dunphy's trial still wasn't going well, despite my inadmissible testimony. He was staring down a life sentence, but now his lawyers are pointing the finger at Gordon as Selena Adams' real killer, and the accusation has created enough reasonable doubt that it's looking like he'll be acquitted."

"Smart," Cam said, and she had to admire his ability to still look at the situation like a cop even though it had hit so close to home. "There's no evidence pointing to Gordon in Selena's death. He'll never be tried for it, and he'll plea his attempted murder sentence down to give up the mastermind behind the contract. He'll be out in a few years and his brother won't spend his life in prison."

Eva nodded. "I don't think Gordon meant to kill you. He wanted it to look good, but if you actually died, he wouldn't be able to get a plea deal. That's why he set the bomb off when Vaughn was half way across the parking lot. He really just wanted to save his brother from a life sentence."

Cam looked over at the closed door of Vaughn's room. "Yeah, I get that. The Dunphys both deserve to rot in hell, but I get it. There's nothing I wouldn't do for my brothers."

"And there's nothing they wouldn't do for you," she said softly.

And silence.

Long, awkward, and chock full of I-don't-wanna-have-this-conversation. At least from his end. And maybe a little from hers, but she wasn't leaving without saying what she needed to say. She thought she'd nearly lost him for good yesterday, and every unspoken word had weighed so heavily on her, breathing had been a chore.

"Is that all you wanted?" he finally asked.

Why had this been so much easier when she thought he was lying injured in that hospital bed?

"No. I want to talk about us." She removed her hand from her pocket. "When I saw—"

He straightened. "Like you said before, there is no *us*."

All the air left her lungs as if he'd hauled off and sucker punched her. "I thought…when you gave me the ring…"

"A moment of foolishness. But I'm done. I can't do this anymore. If you want to be with Preston, go ahead. I hope he makes you happy."

"I don't want Preston. I don't think I ever have, not really." She hesitated, searching for a way to say the things burning a hole in the center of her chest. "I've always wanted what I never got growing up. A real, steady family and—and it's a stupid fantasy, but there was a time that I…" Christ, she was jumbling it all up. So much for her neat list.

"A time that you…what?"

She faltered. Cam didn't lose his patience with anyone— wasn't in his DNA—but irritation laced his tone now. She swallowed to wet her suddenly parched throat.

"Well, I met you several months before I met Preston."

"Yes, your point?"

"And I spent those months hoping for…more. From you. But you never acted like you were interested in me in that way, and Preston worked so hard to win me over…" She blew out a breath. "Preston was convenient and didn't challenge me. With him, I was always in control, and I thought that's what I wanted but—"

"Stop," Cam said, pinching the bridge of his nose. "Eva,

just stop. You don't know what you want."

Outrage had her jaw falling open and burned away her self-doubt. "Excuse me? I know exactly what I want. I'm trying to tell you—"

"No, you don't, and that's the problem. You have this cookie-cutter ideal family in your head, and I don't fit it. Hell, *you* don't fit it, but you refuse to see that. And even if you don't take Linz up on his offer, someone else will eventually come along who you think does fit it, and I'll get regulated to best friend again. I'll grow to hate you for it." He shook his head, and every exhausting second of the past few days showed on his face. "I don't want to hate you when I've spent so many of the past five years in love with you. It'll be easier for everyone if we just end things now."

Her throat tightened and burned. "Easier for everyone, or for you?"

He turned away without answering, but she yanked him around to face her again. "Wilde, dammit, you're not listening to me. I lov—"

Down the hall, the elevator doors opened with a ding and several arguing voices boomeranged off the tile walls, drowning out her voice.

He gazed over her head toward the sound. "My brothers. I have to handle this."

Of course he did.

A strange mix of anger and humiliation bloomed in her chest, and her cheeks heated, no doubt filling with color. At least her face was already so red from the explosion, he wouldn't see the flush.

"Yeah, fine." She dropped her hand from his arm. "Go ahead, indulge your superhero complex. Because everything's absolutely hunky-fucking-dory in our personal life."

"Eva—"

"No, don't." She backed away from him. "I just realized something. I'm not the only one with issues here. But, hey, at least I admit I have control issues, and I'm willing to work through them. You just throw yourself into everyone else's problems and completely ignore your own."

His jaw tightened. "What happened to Vaughn *is* my problem."

"What happened to Vaughn has nothing to do with *us*. That's a whole other can of worms that I'm sure as hell not opening right now, but you're using it as an excuse to push me away. Which is just fucking priceless after all of your talk about wanting me." She struggled to pull his ring off her finger—damn thing was stuck and panic sizzled through her. She didn't want it. Didn't want a reminder of everything they'd had that he was suddenly so willing to toss away.

Finally it popped off over her knuckle and she shoved it at his chest. "We were doomed from the start as friends and as lovers."

Chapter Twenty-Four

Without another word or glance in his direction, Eva stalked past his brothers and jabbed the elevator's down button, then slipped inside when the doors immediately opened. A hollow ache started in his gut and moved to his chest, and he couldn't help but feel like those goddamn metal doors had severed the last remaining thread of friendship between him and Eva as they clamped shut.

He stared down at the ring in his palm. He should go after her, but a fuckton of nasty emotions weighed down his shoulders, keeping his feet planted firmly to the floor.

Christ, it hurt to know his inability to act during those first few months of their acquaintance was the reason she'd gotten together with Preston at all. Hurt even more to know that Preston was the only reason she'd ever come to his bed.

His brothers' voices got louder as they approached, and he stuffed the ring in his jeans pocket. The damn thing all but broadcasted his idiocy, and they sure as shit didn't need to see it.

"I *tried* calling you," Reece was saying. "You ignored me."

Jude, a bit sunburned and still dressed for the tropics, threw out his arms in an act of pure frustration. "Because I thought you were gonna bitch at me for not completing those expense reports before I left. Not because one of our brothers got blown up! Leave a fucking voicemail next time."

"I wouldn't call you about expense reports on your honeymoon," Reece said through clenched teeth, "and I didn't think this was the kind of news to relate via voicemail."

"And finding out from CNN was that much better?" Jude demanded.

"We didn't know it had made national news."

"Car bombs in the nation's capital usually do. And I've spent the last six hours airport-hopping, unable to get a hold of anyone, not knowing how bad Cam was or even if he was alive—"

The break in his youngest brother's voice was the kick in the ass Cam needed, and he gave the argument his full attention. "I'm sorry you had to find out like that."

At the sound of his voice, Jude spotted him, launched forward, and grabbed him in a hard hug. "Holy fuck, you're okay."

"Yeah, I'm fine." He peeled Jude's arms from around his shoulders. "There was a mix-up at the scene—Vaughn was driving my car, not me. But he's going to be fine, too."

"Wait, Vaughn's injured?"

"He's going to be fine," Cam repeated. "A broken leg and ribs, lots of bruises inside and out, lots of swelling. He'll be here for a week or so."

"Okay." Jude sucked in a breath and squeezed his eyes shut for several moments. Steady again, he opened his eyes. "Okay. But I gotta see him. Just to make sure."

Nodding, Cam led the way to Vaughn's room and leaned in to see if his twin was asleep, but Jude, in typical Jude fashion, didn't wait for permission. He shoved inside and stalked to the foot of the bed.

Hands on his hips, he scowled as he studied Vaughn's bruised and battered body. "Hey, asshole. *I'm* supposed to be the troublemaker in the family."

Vaughn's lips stretched into something that might have been a smile if his face wasn't so swollen. "You're a married man now. Libby won't — " He stopped, sucked in a sharp breath, and winced, struggling to shift into a more comfortable position. Cam helped as best he could, stuffing pillows behind Vaughn's back and raising the head of his bed so he sat up straighter, but sweat still rolled down the side of his face and his breathing hitched with the pain. Unfortunately, according to the doctors, he wasn't going to be comfortable again for a long while. And neither was Cam because seeing his twin in so much pain caused a physical ache in the center of his chest that his argument with Eva had not helped.

"Libby won't let you get in trouble anymore," Vaughn continued hoarsely, "so I had to take over the job. Gotta keep Reece and Greer on their toes."

"And you did a helluva job of it." Jude's expression softened and he tapped the end of the bed twice with his palm before going to the door. "I'll be right back."

"Where the hell is he going?" Greer asked.

"I doubt we want to know," Reece said.

Jude returned ten minutes later with a package from the hospital gift shop and tugged on the sheet covering Vaughn's legs. "Now I believe Cam mentioned a cast…"

Vaughn groaned. "Don't you dare. I'll make you bleed."

"You couldn't make a hemophiliac bleed right now, bro." With a grin, he produced a ten-pack of neon markers from the gift shop bag. "And I'm thinking you need a pretty pink unicorn on your cast."

All five of them spent the evening together in Vaughn's room, eating a dinner of delivered Chinese and vending machine soda. Reece demolished his General Tso's in no time, then began flipping through news channels on TV, no doubt already running financial figures and damage analysis in his computer-like brain, trying to figure out how they would salvage their business when half of their building had been blown to ruins. Greer sat in a second visitor chair, aged a decade by exhaustion and worry, picking at his lo mein with a pair of chopsticks. Jude skipped dinner and continued drawing on Vaughn's cast, finishing the unicorn and peppering the top of his foot with hearts and swirls. Nobody spoke, but as usual, their memories of a better time filled the silence—the eight-hundred pound gorilla in the room that everyone studiously ignored.

Still, it was kind of nice to be all together for a meal. Minus the hospital and take out cartons, it was almost like a real sit-down family dinner. Or at least as close as the Wilde brothers had gotten to one since before their parents died.

A bittersweet longing filled Cam's chest as he poked at

his moo goo gai pan. He thought of Eva's idea of a family, then thought of his own parents. He'd had that ideal once and it had been shattered by a senseless act of violence. Maybe that was why he just couldn't bring himself to believe in the kind of future Eva wanted.

The murder of their parents had impacted each of the brothers in different ways. Jude had become insolent. Vaughn, reckless. Reece, callous. Greer, detached. And Cam? What had he become? He had no idea, but suspected it wasn't something he was happy with.

They'd lost the foundation of their family that cold October night twenty years ago, but had gained the kind of forged-in-battle bond usually seen in brothers-in-arms rather than in true blooded brothers. Cam saw that bond now, so tangible he could almost touch it, but still took little comfort from it. He had his brothers, yes, but, dammit all, he *wanted* the kind of family Eva talked about. The real thing, the kind that sat down to meals together every night and chatted about their days. The kind who celebrated holidays and birthdays with more than a beer and a slap on the back.

Didn't matter now.

He'd been such a goddamn pussy, carrying a flame for her all these years, unable to be honest about what he wanted with her from the get-go. He didn't want friendship. Never had, but the thought of loving and losing her had made him keep his distance. And his silence had pushed her straight into Preston Linz's arms. Hell, breaking his silence after all these years had probably accomplished the exact same thing.

Cam didn't think he'd ever forgive himself for that.

Looking at Vaughn laying in the hospital bed, so bruised

and swollen, he realized he had a lot that he wasn't going to forgive himself for and lost his appetite.

By the time visiting hours ended, Vaughn's cast looked like the pages of a teenage girl's notebook. He promised creative, humiliating revenge, and everyone—even Cam—laughed. It took Vaughn feigning sleepiness for Greer, Reece, and Jude to start making noises about leaving and another fifteen minutes before they actually cleared out.

But as soon as the door shut behind them, Vaughn's eyes popped open, and he nailed Cam with his *spill it* glare. "Want to explain to me what that was all about?"

Cam jerked a thumb over his shoulder, indicating the door. "Jude was pissed because—"

"Not that. Eva. You know exactly what she was trying to tell you by wearing that ring."

Dropping heavily into the seat Reece had vacated, Cam dragged both hands over his head. "I know."

"And you are stupid in love with her. So explain to me why you're sitting here instead of annoying our neighbors with rowdy make-up sex?"

"Because…I can't."

Vaughn hissed through his teeth. "That's probably something you should get checked, bro."

"Jesus. If you weren't already down and out, I'd punch you."

"Nah, you wouldn't. You know I'm right about this." He yawned. Maybe he wasn't faking sleepiness after all.

Cam stood to make tracks and let him get some rest, but Vaughn pointed a finger at him, pinning him in his place. "Hold it."

"Bro, you're exhausted. I'll be back tomorrow."

"Nope. Sit your ass back down."

Cam sat. "Now you sound like Greer."

"Good. I'll take that as a compliment." He paused to shut his eyes and let his ragged breathing from the strain of so much movement even out. Just as Cam started wondering if he could make an escape before Vaughn gathered his strength, he opened his eyes again.

"You recall me saying you're stupid in love? Emphasis on *stupid*. That fight you and Eva had in the hall was almost as painful to listen to as the rest of my injuries."

Yeah, he wasn't going to sit still for a lecture on relationships from *Vaughn* of all people. His twin's idea of long-term started and ended with one-night-stand. "Vaughn, I love you, but stay the hell out of my business."

"No, I'm not done. So she used you to get over her ex? Boo-fucking-hoo. You enjoyed every second of being used and if she hadn't, she never would have come to the conclusion that she did."

"What, that I have a superhero complex?"

"Well, yeah, you do."

He strode to the door. "All right. I'm outta here."

"Camden," Vaughn said in exasperation behind him. "She loves you. And you know I don't say this lightly, but I like her for you. Don't throw away the best thing you've ever had."

*B*est thing he'd ever had.

Vaughn's lecture haunted him throughout the taxi ride home and followed him around the too-empty condo until he couldn't stand it anymore and stepped outside. He needed a ride, couldn't keep relying on taxis or his brothers, and he hadn't even looked at the insurance paperwork for his toasted 4Runner yet. So, with nothing more than a flashlight and the icy wind for company, he set about finally fixing the Hummer's slashed tire and hoped the busy work would keep him from thinking too much.

He was wrong.

Best thing he'd ever had.

The words rattled around in his skull as he removed the ruined tire and tossed it into the snow, then fit the spare in its place.

Yeah, no doubt about it. Eva was the best thing in his life. But right now, she was also the worst. Every cell in his being screamed at him that she was his—even as pissed off as he was at her, his body ached for the soft, tight heat of hers—but she didn't see it. She couldn't see it, or she'd have thrown Preston's ring back at him the moment he tried to give it to her. Instead, she kept it. Even considered his proposal.

A more rational part of him got that this was all his fault. She'd only agreed to see Preston again because she was angry at him. He'd betrayed her trust. And after he'd sworn to himself he wouldn't.

Cam released the tire jack, slid it out of the way, and yanked open the Hummer's door hard enough that the hinges protested. The screech of sound dragged him out of his head, and he realized he'd also been grinding his teeth the entire time he changed the tire.

Jesus Christ.

He slid into the driver's seat and leaned his forehead against the cool steering wheel. Opened and closed his mouth a few times to work the ache out of his jaw, and then just sat there, breathing. Each exhale clouded in the cold, but he didn't switch on the behemoth excuse for an SUV because anger and fear burned in equal parts beneath his skin.

Fear?

Holy shit. That was exactly the emotion clouding his every thought right now. He was so damn afraid he'd lose Eva somewhere down the line like he'd lost his parents, like he'd nearly lost Vaughn yesterday. But instead of grabbing and holding on to her with everything he had in him, he'd shoved her away.

Cam banged his forehead against the wheel, once, twice, three times. Idiot, idiot, idiot. Groaning at himself, he sat up and cranked the ignition. He had to go talk to her.

Man, Vaughn called it right: *Stupid* in love.

Chapter Twenty-Five

Eva had been shaking with anger since she left the hospital. What the hell did Cam know about her ideal family anyway? And fuck him for that comment about her not knowing what she wanted. She knew exactly what she wanted and she would have told him if the dumbass had just closed his mouth and listened.

She'd also been banging things around her mess of a kitchen for the last hour, not really accomplishing much in the way of cleaning, but the clang of pots and pans against the sink was satisfying. Maybe she could use one to beat some sense into Cam's head.

Now there was a satisfying thought.

Still, she should probably do some actual cleaning. Shelby was away for a few days, visiting their mother at the psychiatric institute in Virginia—God knows why she even bothered after what happened between them—but Eva might as well take advantage of her sister's absence and put the house back in order. Besides, the monotony of chores might help her find her Zen place so she could deal with Cam tomorrow on an even keel.

And she would deal with him. This thing between them was far from finished.

Somewhat steadier, Eva started unloading the dishes she'd tossed in the sink. Some of them looked clean already, but she'd been so pissed off she hadn't paid any attention to whether the plates stacked on the counter had been clean or dirty, so they were all getting washed. She stoppered the sink and turned on the water as hot as she could stand it, then added a few squirts of dish soap.

The doorbell rang.

Cam?

Her heart did a funny jitter thing.

She left the sink to fill and strode into the living room, grabbing her side arm from the closet on the way. Just in case. A woman home alone could be too much of a temptation to some desperate criminal, and it was late enough at night that she didn't feel one-hundred percent safe opening the door without her gun. She checked the peep hole, her heart now threatening to gallop out of her chest at the thought of having it out with Cam tonight—

Preston.

Sighing, she tucked her weapon into her waistband and pulled her shirt out to cover it. Unlike Cam, Preston wouldn't get why she'd answered the door with it, which was just another reason in a long list of many why it'd never work between them. Why it took her so long to figure that out, she didn't know. She'd kick herself for it later.

She opened the door and barely got a squeak of sound

out before he pulled her into his arms.

"I'm so sorry," he breathed into her hair, and his hands roamed a little too far down her back for comfort.

"For what?" She ducked out of his embrace and ignored his stricken expression.

"You haven't heard? It's all over the major news stations. I thought…with him being your best friend…"

"Oh. Cam." She wasn't sure how she felt about him being here just because he thought Cam was in the hospital.

He wrapped his arms around her again. "I'm so sorry. I'll admit I never liked Camden, but I can't imagine what you're going through right now. I'm here for you, okay? Anything you need."

"What are you—Cam's fine." She shoved at his shoulders until he backed up a step. "*Vaughn* got hurt, but he's going to be okay."

"Vaughn?"

"Yeah. Cam's twin?"

He blinked like he had no idea what she was talking about. She planted her hands on her hips and stared in complete amazement. "Wow, you really didn't listen to me much when we were together."

Yet another reason their relationship wouldn't have worked.

For the first time, she saw Preston Linz without the filter of her idealism, and she wasn't liking what she saw. Preston put on a good act, but he only cared for one person: himself.

"Twin?" he said through his teeth. "There's *two* of him?"

"Of course not. They're two completely separate people who happen to look alike. What the fuck's wrong with you? You're acting like—Oh, shit. The sink!" She left him standing in the open doorway and ran back to the kitchen, catching the faucet just in time before the basin overflowed with water. The bubbles were another matter. They had multiplied like rabbits and spilled over onto the counter and floor.

Cursing, she plunged her hand into the scalding water to find the plug and felt Preston at her back, uncomfortably close.

His breath rustled the hair by her ear. "Were you fucking them both?"

She jerked backwards in shock, but found his body behind hers, pinning her against the sink.

"Because Camden's been fucking both you and Lark."

But at least we both figured out the kind of man he was before we made any stupid mistakes, right?

Eva's heart pumped double time, spilling adrenaline into her blood. Lark had been in Vaughn's hospital room. Only one reason she'd have gone to see him. They had some kind of relationship—and Preston thought Vaughn was Cam.

Oh, no.

The contract on Cam's head. Soup's death. All of it started after Preston saw her and Cam together at the bar in Key West.

A rising sense of dread trickled down her spine. "Preston, tell me you didn't—" But she didn't get the chance to finish her sentence. An engine rumbled to a stop in front of the house and a car door banged shut. Footsteps crunched on the snow of the walkway, then the porch's screen door creaked. She'd left the interior door open, and the footsteps paused.

Please not Shelby. Or—

Cam appeared in the archway between the dining room

and kitchen, his gun drawn, his eyes flat as he took in the scene in front of him: Preston pinning her against the sink with his body, her shirt soaked down the front, the white fabric translucent.

For one horrifying moment, Eva feared he'd get the wrong idea, but Preston nixed that by grabbing a knife out of the butcher block. He pressed the blade to her neck and swung her around, using her as a living shield, and her whole body went cold. Her brain shut down. She couldn't form a coherent thought, leaving her confused and shaking.

"Whoa, okay. We don't need to hurt anyone." Cam raised his hands in front of him, let his gun dangle from his index finger as he bent down and set it on the floor. Straightening, he stripped off his jacket, then his shirt. "I'm unarmed, see? No back-up weapons."

He continued to speak to Preston in calm, soothing tones, and his voice served as a beacon in a sea of darkness for her to focus on. She heard her name. Once, twice. The kitchen came back into focus, slowly at first, then in such sharp relief, it gave her a headache.

"Eva," Cam said, "you okay? Eva?"

"Y-yes." The knife bit into her skin, but seeing Cam acting so calm relaxed her enough that she was able to think again. Control. She needed to get control, even if it was only over the way she died. She swallowed, felt the knife's edge dig deeper, and ignored it. "Yes, I'm fine. Preston hired our bomber. I think he may have killed Soup, too."

"Damn junkie should have done his job in the first place," Preston said. "All he had to do was get Camden out of my way. Instead, he took my money and ran. I couldn't let that stand."

Cam nodded. "Yeah, but like you said, Soup was a junkie. Nobody cares about him, right?"

"Exactly," Preston said.

"The car bomb didn't kill anyone and Gordon Dunphy will go down for that. You're smart. We can't prove you were involved in anything—except for this. Right here, right now. But you're smart, right, Preston? You get that if you hurt Eva tonight, you will get caught. She's a cop. Assault an officer of the law, that's a long prison sentence. Murder an officer, that's automatic life."

"I'm not going to hurt her. I want her to make a decision. The *right* decision."

"She already has." Cam turned his pockets inside out and held up the ruby-studded ring. His gaze locked on hers. "She gave this back to me tonight."

Preston's breath grazed her ear again and she shuddered in revulsion. "Is that true?"

"Go ahead," Cam prompted. "Tell him what you told me."

She opened her mouth to play along, but stopped. There Cam stood, bare chested, his pockets turned inside out, the ring he'd bought for her in his hand, and a plea in his eyes. Outwardly, he appeared calm, but she saw the terror trembling through him—and she couldn't do it. She couldn't choose Preston over him, not even to save her life. She held his gaze, saw his eyes widen.

No, Cam mouthed. *Don't.*

"I love you, Cam. I'll always pick you."

O h fuck.
  Cam launched across the kitchen as Preston let out an inhuman howl of rage, and the knife dug into her neck. Eva dropped to her knees and—

Blood. So much blood.

No, no, no. He couldn't be too late.

Except she was moving, sweeping out her leg, knocking Preston's from under him. He stumbled backwards, and Cam caught him in a tackle around the middle, shoving him into the scalding water in the sink. The guy screamed, the sound carrying up though the water and bubbles.

"Cuffs!" Cam said and Eva scrambled out of the kitchen, slipping and sliding until she hit the dry linoleum of the dining room.

Preston bucked, slashed out with the knife, and caught Cam's bare chest with the edge, but he shoved the asshole's head under the water again. He knocked Preston's hand against the counter until the knife dropped, then kicked it out of the way and hauled Preston away from the sink, flattening him out on the kitchen floor.

Eva returned with the handcuffs, handed them over, then pulled her gun from her waistband and pointed it at the back of Preston's head. "Don't fucking move." To Cam, "I called this in."

"All right." He snapped the cuffs around Preston's wrists, but kept the majority of his weight on the man as he finally looked up at Eva. She had a decent gash in the side of her neck. Wasn't deep enough to be life-threatening, but she was bleeding down the front of her soaked T-shirt. Her chest heaved, her entire body trembled, but she still managed to hold the gun steady.

She noticed him checking her over and her eyes softened. "I'm okay, Cam."

Yeah. His strong, capable Eva—of course she was okay. Or at least she would be once she got that wound treated. He drummed up a smile. "Nice moves. Recognized that leg trick."

"You should. I've taken you down with it enough."

"Got it figured out now. You won't get me next time."

As sirens drew closer outside, she grinned at him. "Wanna bet?"

Chapter Twenty-Six

"Lark's missing."

Eva released a pent up breath and wrapped her cold hands around the coffee Cam set on the desk in front of her. After giving her statement, she'd taken a hot shower in the police department's locker room and changed into a fresh pair of clothes she kept in her locker, but she still couldn't shake the cold numbing her to the center of her being. The news only deepened the icy feeling, making her shiver even though it wasn't completely unexpected. She'd sent officers to Lark's home as soon as they had Preston in custody. "I was afraid of that."

Cam propped a hip on the edge of the desk, just like the old days when they had discussed cases late into the night. "The going theory is Preston killed her when she rejected him for Vaughn, but there's no sign of blood in her apartment. No body. He won't say what he did with her."

"I saw her at the hospital yesterday afternoon." And

suddenly, that encounter made a whole lot more sense. She'd gone to see Vaughn, which explained why she was so confused when Eva spoke about him as if he was Cam. "Does Vaughn know?"

"Yeah." He scrubbed his face with both hands. "He didn't take it well. He cared about her, more than I've seen him care about any of the women he's dated."

"I had no idea they were even together until Preston told me. Except, he thought Vaughn was you."

"Nobody knew. They kept it secret, but it started in Key West."

She nodded, so weighted down by exhaustion even that small action was a chore. "And Preston lost his mind when she dumped him for another Wilde."

Cam hesitated. He tried to cover by taking a drink of his own coffee, but she knew him, inside and out. She glared at him. "What?"

Sighing, he set his mug aside. "Preston didn't lose his mind in Key West. That's just when he fixated on killing me and started using his political affiliations to track down people I'd arrested who held grudges. Except he made a big mistake by approaching Soup. Yeah, I arrested Soup once, and we had a rocky start to our acquaintance, but he liked me, considered me a friend. Friendship is something beyond Preston's understanding."

Eva nodded, knowing he spoke the truth. But if he was aiming to comfort her, he failed. She didn't feel any freaking better about the whole thing. "You're stalling. How do you know Preston didn't snap in Key West?"

"He's doing a lot of talking in there." With a tilt of his head, Cam indicated the interrogation room, where Miguel and another detective were interviewing Preston. "It all still has to be substantiated, but he's confessed to killing at least three women, starting as far back as his first girlfriend in high school. He doesn't take rejection well."

She shivered harder. Oh, God, how could she have known him for five years, dated him for two, and not once suspected…

Dammit, she should have seen something. As a cop, her job was to protect the innocent, and instead, she'd literally been in bed with one of the bad guys. Sickness roiled in her stomach, and she feared she might throw up the little bit of coffee she'd drank. She clamped her jaw shut and fought to rein in all of her bodily reactions. She had to maintain control. She was too close to an emotional cliff, and if she let go of the reins on her emotions, she'd tremble over the edge.

Cam growled and stood, pulling her to her feet and tucking her against his chest. "Goddamn you, Eva. You don't have to be strong right now. Nobody fucking expects that of you except yourself. Let go. Break down. Get it out of your system."

She balled her fists in his shirt, but didn't lift her face from the crook of his neck. "If I start, I won't stop."

"Then don't." His hand caressed the back of her head, tangled in the strands of her hair, and pulled gently until she had to meet his gaze. "I'm here for you. I'll always be here for you."

As she stared up into the serious blue of his eyes, she saw the truth of his words. From that first day when he leaned across this very aisle and offered her a carrot stick, he'd had her back, saved her ass, and had just been there for her.

She *could* let go because Cam would always be there to

catch her and set her back on her feet, no matter how far she fell.

Wrapping her arms around his waist, she leaned into his strength and let the tears come.

Eva's tears destroyed him, but he held her through it, wishing he could absorb her pain, until she finally cried herself into exhaustion. Then he bundled her into the Hummer and drove her home—his home, where she belonged. She moved like a zombie, silent, unblinking, and unconcerned of her surroundings as he led her up the steps to his condo. Fearing she might collapse, he scooped her into his arms the moment the door shut out the cold behind them. The fact she allowed it without protest worried the hell outta him, and he double-timed it to his bedroom.

He pulled back the sheets and gently laid her on the mattress, unsurprised to see her already out cold. Couldn't blame her. The night had packed a huge wallop—both physical and emotional. At very least, she needed a solid night's sleep.

He stripped out of his clothes and slid into bed beside her, tucked her in against his chest. She sighed and nuzzled closer in her sleep. His muscles loosened, his heart beat easier, his lungs expanded for what felt like the first time since walking into her house and seeing that knife held to her throat.

She was safe. In his arms and safe. And fuck their friends-with-benefits arrangement with all its rules, he was never letting her go again.

Eva woke nestled in bed with Cam's even, sleeping breaths rustling her hair. For several disorientated moments, she couldn't remember how she end up here, but didn't care all that much because his arms were warm around her, his heartbeat comforting under her ear.

Then, as the fuzziness of sleep cleared, memories of last night seeped back. She reached up and traced the edge of the bandage on her neck. Yes, the whole thing had been real. Damn. She kind of hoped it had all been a terrifying dream.

The movement woke Cam, and his arms tightened around her. She smiled into his neck. "Your shoulder's gotta be asleep by now."

"Yup," he agreed but made no move to release her.

"Why don't you let me go?"

In a surge of movement, he changed positions and tucked her underneath him, his thighs trapping hers. "Never," he said and dipped his head.

His lips, gentle on hers, stirred up a hot need low in her belly. She threaded her fingers through his hair and tugged him down, demanding more. He indulged her, treating her to lingering kisses that stoked the fire burning within her.

Christ, she'd missed him.

His big hand traced the outline of her body, found the edge of her shirt, and pushed it up, exposing her bare skin. He broke away from her lips and slid lower, trailing kisses down her body. She arched toward his mouth and felt his lips curve as he nuzzled her lower belly.

"Still want that cookie cutter family?" he asked, working

his way down her body. "Two-point-five kids, a minivan, a dog?"

"Hmm. That sounds…" Realization had her bolting upright, nearly knocking Cam in the chin with her knee. "Really fucking dull. I don't want a dog. I want a parrot. And I'd rather get a root canal than be caught driving a minivan."

Cam sat up, his hair rumpled and eyes hooded. "That so?"

"Yes, and I do want kids. A couple at least. And I still want them to have family dinners—most nights—and college funds. I want them to have a father they can rely on, who will always be there for them." She leaned forward and cupped his cheeks in her hands. "And I very much want you to be their father, but I'm afraid I can't trust myself to make this kind of decision anymore. My taste in men is as bad as my mother's."

"Hey," he said, offended.

"I'm sorry, but I've known Preston for as long as I've known you. I thought I really *knew* him, and look how that turned out."

"Because he's a liar," Cam pointed out. "A slick, professional liar who charmed his way past a lot of people's defenses. You only saw the face he wanted you to see, the one he thought would be most attractive to you."

She knew he was speaking the truth. That's how serial killers operate. They lead double lives, showing the world a socially acceptable face while their victims are the only witnesses to their true evil. And yet… "How can I be sure I'm not making the same mistake with you?"

Cam removed her hands from his face and kissed each of her knuckles before twining his fingers through hers. "What was Preston's favorite color?"

She blinked. "Um. Blue? I think."

"Mine?"

"Red, same as mine. But that doesn't prove anything."

"His favorite food?" he persisted.

"He…" She searched her memory and came up blank. "I guess he never said."

"Mine?"

"Baby carrots with a little bit of ranch dressing to dip them in."

"His favorite sport?"

"Maybe…baseball? He took me to a few Nationals games, but…" When she trailed off, Cam tilted his head in a *go on* gesture. She sighed, seeing exactly where he was going with all this. "He spent most of the time on his phone and never paid much attention to the games."

"Uh-huh. And my favorite sport?" Cam prompted.

"Hockey. You love the Caps, which is so sad because they always choke during playoffs."

He smiled and shook his head in exasperation, but her calculated jab didn't do its job and get him to change subjects. "What about my worst habit?"

His tone was all challenge now and the knots bunching up the muscles between her shoulders eased out. "Biting your nails. You started doing it after you stopped smoking."

"Which was how long ago?"

"Shortly before we met. You quit cold turkey after eight years as a social smoker."

He nodded. "My biggest fear?"

Eva started to answer with a silly and arbitrary fear—his dislike of clowns jumped to mind—but then closed her mouth without uttering a sound. Yeah, clowns spooked him and so did Shark Week on Discovery Channel, which she'd always found hilarious, but that was not the kind of fear he meant. He was talking about something deeper, the kind of fear that dictated a person's every thought and action. And the fact she understood his question without clarification— and knew its answer—told her oodles about how solid the foundation of their relationship was. She'd never be able to answer such a question about Preston because she didn't know him at his core. Thank God. Getting a glimpse into the man's twisted soul would have left her scarred for life. As it was, she'd be doubting her instincts for a long time to come.

But Cam? He was a good man, through and through. She'd always been able to trust him with her life when they worked together. Before last night, she'd already decided to trust him with her heart. And, dammit, she refused to let Preston take that goodness away from her.

Eva closed the distance between them and brushed a light kiss over his mouth. "You're most afraid of losing your brothers, which is one of your best qualities even though it makes you do stupid things like lie to them."

"Not only my brothers," he said softly, reaching out to tuck a strand of hair behind her ear. "You, too. I've lived every day of the past five years terrified that I'll wake up and you'll be gone from my life, and that has stopped me from having the kind of relationship I've always wanted with you. But no more. Eva, I love you. My life isn't worth the air I breathe without you in it, and if that means I risk losing you someday…well, that's a risk I'm more than willing to take."

An incandescent joy settled low in her belly and lit her up from the inside out.

"I love you, too, Cam, and I'm not going anywhere." Swallowing back a lump of emotion, she poked his bare chest. "And I'd like my ring back since I have every intention of marrying you."

His dimple flashed as he pushed off the bed, found his pants on the floor, and dug the ring out of the pocket. Returning to her side, he held it up and its rubies glittered in the pale morning light from the window. "Our life won't be sitcom perfect, but I promise whatever life we make together will be perfect for us."

Tears gathered in her eyes as he slid the ring on her finger, and for once, she didn't try to stop them. He leaned in and caught the droplets with his lips. Her pulse kicked, spilling a heady mix of love and desire through her blood. She tilted her head back, inviting his lips to explore. Against her leg, his erection swelled and lengthened, and she wrapped her hand around him, stroked him until a growl thrummed from his chest.

She sighed. "Make love to me, Cam."

"Absolutely." He nudged her down on the bed, drawing off her shirt, then her pants and panties in one pull as he sat back on his knees. His gaze swept down her, all heat and worship, and a wave of goose bumps rose in its wake.

"Are you wet for me?" He shoved his own pants off and his erection sprang free, long and hard, straining toward her. He took himself in one hand while the fingers of his other teased her entrance until she was ready to detonate.

"Yes. Oh, yes." She pressed against his hand and his thumb on her clit sent shockwaves rippling outward. Oh, she was close. So, so close. "Please, Cam. I want you inside me."

"Fuck, yeah." He lifted her hips and joined them together in a hard thrust, tearing a moan from her throat.

But once fully seated inside her, he stopped moving.

He leaned forward, braced his weight on his forearms, and swept his lips reverently over her eyelids, cheeks, then finally her mouth.

When she opened her eyes, he grinned down at her. "Want a big, traditional wedding with all the frills?"

Her laugh caught in her throat. "Is that your idea of a marriage proposal?"

"It's my idea of wedding plans." He circled his hips, his pelvis hit just the right spot, and her muscles seized in pleasure. He held her through the orgasm, murmuring in her ear, telling her exactly how good it felt for him when she came, and the dirty talk only intensified her climax.

As the tremors subsided, she wrapped her arms around him. "I don't think so. How about Vegas?"

He froze and stared at her as if seeing her for the first time. "Really?"

"Yes. It's not perfect, but it's perfect for us." She stroked her hands down his back, tightened her legs around him. "When can we leave?"

His hips jerked. "How about as soon as we finish here? In, let's say…a week. If we can both still walk."

"You can't keep me in bed for a week."

"Yeah?" He withdrew from her, then sank in again, and her eyes nearly rolled back in her head. He chuckled. "Wanna bet?"

She smiled and opened to him, accepting him deeper into her body and her heart. Her partner, her best friend, her lover. Very soon, he'd also be her husband. And, someday, the father of her children.

Which, she decided, was a damn excellent benefit to their friendship.

About the Author

Writing has always been Tonya's one true love. She wrote her first novel-length story in 8th grade and hasn't put down her pen since. She received a B.A. in creative writing from SUNY Oswego and is now working on an MFA in popular fiction at Seton Hill University.

Tonya shares her life with two dogs and a ginormous cat. They live in a small town in Pennsylvania, but she suffers from a bad case of wanderlust and usually ends up moving someplace new every few years. Luckily, her animals are all excellent travel buddies.

When Tonya is not writing, she spends her time reading, painting, exploring new places, and enjoying time with her family.

www.tonyaburrows.com

Discover the **Wilde Security** *series…*

WILDE NIGHTS IN PARADISE
a *Wilde Security* novel by Tonya Burrows

Former Marine Jude Wilde's motto has always been "burn bridges and never look back." But when Wilde Security is hired to protect district attorney Libby Pruitt, the woman he loved and left, Jude can't ignore the heat—or the animosity—sparking between them. With her life on the line and a grudge to break, can he win back Libby's heart?

Discover the HORNET series by Tonya Burrows

SEAL OF HONOR

HONOR RECLAIMED

BROKEN HONOR

66060657R00156

Made in the USA
Lexington, KY
02 August 2017